SPELLHOUND

A Dragons of Hallow book

SPELLHOUND

A Dragons of Hallow book

LIAN TANNER

Illustrated by Sally Soweol Han

ALLEN&UNWIN

SYDNEY · MELBOURNE · AUCKLAND · LONDON

First published by Allen & Unwin in 2023

Allen & Unwin
Cammeraygal Country
83 Alexander Street
Crows Nest NSW 2065
Australia
Phone: (61 2) 8425 0100
Email: info@allenandunwin.com
Web: www.allenandunwin.com

*Allen & Unwin acknowledges the Traditional Owners of the Country
on which we live and work. We pay our respects to all Aboriginal
and Torres Strait Islander Elders, past and present.*

 A catalogue record for this
book is available from the
National Library of Australia

ISBN 978 1 76118 005 7

For teaching resources, explore
www.allenandunwin.com/resources/for-teachers

Cover and text design by Hannah Janzen
Cover illustration by Sally Soweol Han
Set in Bembo 12.5/17pt by Hannah Janzen

10 9 8 7 6 5 4 3 2 1

www.liantanner.com.au
www.sallyhanillustration.com

*To my uber wonderful and uber
talented writing group:
Deb, Sarah, Tristan and Zanni*

In a quiet corner of Hallow, far from cities and towns, roads and railways, walls and witches, there lived a family of Spellhounds.

Of course you have never heard of Spellhounds. They are one of the Three Great Secrets of Hallow, a country that loves secrets almost as much as it loves green jellybabies.

The First Great Secret is that Queen Felicia, beloved ruler of Hallow, is ████████

The Second Great Secret is ████████████ ████████████████████

The Third Great Secret is the Spellhounds.

What? No, I'm not going to tell you anything more about them. I am a loyal citizen of Hallow, and would never betray—

Oh, you have jellybabies?

Green ones?

Well, I suppose I could tell you a *little* more.

But first you must promise not to whisper it to anyone else. Not even your best friend. Not even your dog.

Especially not your dog.

Do you promise?

All right then. Come closer. Open your ears and your heart, and pass the green jellybabies.

I will tell you a story about the Spellhounds.

CHAPTER 1
An Ordinary Minch-wiggin

But first I must tell you about the minch-wiggin.

Her name was Flax, and she was completely ordinary.

Well, except for her whiskers, which glowed in the dark. And her bare feet, which sometimes struck sparks from the floor of the Floating Forest.

And except for the small, sharp sword she carried in a sheath across her back, next to a leather satchel.

Minch-wiggins do not usually carry swords. So you would expect Flax to be proud of hers. After all, it had been passed down from her great-great-great-great-great-great-great-great-great-great-great-great-great-great-great-great-great-great-grandmother. And it made her *very* important.

But right now, it was getting in her way.

She would have taken it off and laid it under a tree. But if she did, one of her cousins might come along and find it. They wouldn't dare touch it. But they would set up a great squeaking, loud enough to be heard from one end of the Floating Forest to the other.

'I have found Flaxseed's sword, but there is no sign of Flax,' they would squeak. 'The dragon must have eaten her. Help! Disaster! We are doomed!'

And before she could shout down from the piplum tree that she was *right here* above their heads, and that the dragon hadn't been seen in the Floating Forest for at least a hundred years, every minch-wiggin in Minchfold would be in a panic.

The minch-wiggin babies chasing each other along the branches would freeze with terror. Their fathers and mothers would drop the nuts and seeds they had painstakingly gathered, scoop up the babies and dive into the nearest nest. The grandmothers, grandfathers, aunties and uncles would grab anyone left behind and tumble in after them.

The noisy bustling trees of Minchfold, which were filled with magic from root to twig, would fall silent. But the ropes and vines and swings would tremble with fear, and so would every one of Flax's people.

Flax didn't want them to tremble. So she kept the sword on her back, next to the leather satchel.

And, as the forest birds sang up the dawn, and the frogs croaked, and the horned globs moaned, she worried under her breath.

'I wish it hadn't been me,' she whispered as she strung a rope woven from the finest spider silk across the path. 'I wish Grandpa had given the sword to my brother Bean, or to Cousin Violet.'

But he hadn't. He'd passed it to Flax on his deathbed, when everyone was watching. So she'd had no choice. She'd had to take it.

She snipped off another piece of rope with her teeth and strung it next to the first, using her black-tipped tail for balance.

A third rope went across the first two. And a fourth, and a fifth. Despite the sword, Flax worked quickly. It was nearly sunrise, and she wanted to have the web finished before the sun touched the treetops.

'I wish I'd dropped the sword,' she whispered. 'I wish I'd squeaked, "Oops, butter-fingers!" and dropped it on the floor. Then Bean or Violet would have picked it up, and the satchel as well. And *they* would be Destroyer-of-Dragons-and-Protector-of-her-People instead of me. I'm sure they'd be much better at it.'

She tied an extra strong rope to the edge of the web. She took the other end of the rope in her hand, scrambled down from the tree and hid in a pile of leaves at the side of the path.

And she waited for the wild magic to come.

Flax had strong legs for climbing, and strong

fingers for plucking seeds and peeling acorns. She had a black-tipped tail for holding on to branches. She was quick and nimble.

But wild magic was even quicker. It darted along the forest paths so fast that Flax could never catch it without a web.

So she crouched among the leaves. And she waited.

Alone. But not *quite* alone.

Beside her squatted a Secret.

A Dark and Terrible Secret.

No, I'm not going to tell you what it was.

Why not? Because this is a story. And it has to be told in the right order.

CHAPTER 2
The Spellhound Pup

Flax was not the only one with a Dark and Terrible Secret.

On the far side of the Floating Forest, the Spellhound pup should have been in a warm, snoring huddle, draped over his mother and father in the sleeping den.

Instead, he was right up at the back of the den, near the tree roots.

By himself.

His parents had lain awake all night, worrying about him. Their quiet voices still drifted along the tunnel to his ears.

'I'm sure there's something wrong with him,'

his mother said, for the tenth or eleventh time.

She's right, the pup thought miserably (for the tenth or eleventh time). *There* is *something wrong with me.*

'Maybe it's just growing pains,' said his father.

'He had growing pains when the moon was full,' growled his mother. 'I know what growing pains smell like. This is something else.'

The pup wriggled uncomfortably. And for the *hundred* and tenth, or *hundred* and eleventh time, he wondered if he should just crawl down the tunnel and tell his parents the truth.

Should he have told them?

Of course he should.

Would they still have loved him?

Of course they would.

But despite his great size, he was just a pup, and did not yet understand how love works.

So he stayed where he was.

His parents' voices trailed away into sleep. The pup slept too, dreaming of storm clouds...

And then, suddenly, he was awake.

Something was wrong. A smell had drifted into the den.

A *new* smell.

A scorching, *dangerous* smell!

The pup scrambled to his feet. A whimper escaped him, and he felt his mother and father jolt awake.

Outside the den, something **GROOOWLED!**

It was not the sort of growl that belonged in the Floating Forest. It sounded bigger than the pup's father. (And *nothing* was bigger than him!)

It sounded more ferocious than the pup's mother. (And *no one* was more ferocious than her!)

The pup froze in terror.

Something was digging at the entrance to the den. Something huge—

'Run, my child!' howled the pup's mother. 'RUN!'

'RUUUUUUUUUUN!' howled his mother and father together.

The pup squeezed between the tree roots. He dug frantically at the thin wall of earth that hid the escape tunnel.

He burst out into the dim light.

He ran.

CHAPTER 3
Something in the Forest

Flax crouched under the leaves, waiting for the magic to come.

To fill the time, she cleaned her fingernails with a piplum thorn. She groomed the tip of her tail. She sang an old song about blueberries and beechnuts.

Halfway through the second verse, she stopped.

One of the dawn-singing birds had fallen silent.

Flax knew every part of the Floating Forest. She knew where the owls slept, and where the sketters lurked. She knew the exact time of year when mor-kits grew their hunting teeth, and where the best acorns could be found, and the sweetest streams, and where the magic danced and sang and whispered.

She knew when there was something in the forest that didn't belong.

Another bird stopped singing. And another. The frogs stopped croaking. The horned globs no longer moaned.

Even the trees seemed to be holding their breath.

Every hair on Flax's body stood on end. *Danger*, she thought. *DANGER!*

She peered up at the sky, hoping with all her heart that the dragon hadn't come.

She couldn't see anything. She couldn't hear anything, except the dreadful silence.

But she kept watching the sky, right up until—

Right up until something HUGE and BLACK and MONSTROUS blundered down the path – straight through her carefully woven web – and kept running.

Flax was so shocked that she forgot to let go of the rope. And by the time she got her wits back, she was being dragged through the forest so fast that she didn't *dare* let go.

Trees flashed past. Sketters, horned globs and vicious little mor-kits dived for cover. Owls, wrens and fluffy drongos took to the sky in a fluster of feathers.

Flax hung on desperately, with the sword and the satchel bouncing on her back.

Was this the dragon? Was this the monster she was supposed to destroy?

Eek! she thought. *Eeeeeeeeeeeeeeeeeek!*

She jammed her eyes shut. The monster had to stop soon. Or at least slow down. And when it did, she would drop the rope, dive under the nearest bush and pretend to be a stick.

But the monster didn't stop. It kept running and running—

Until it came to the edge of the Floating Forest.

What, you didn't realise the Floating Forest would have an edge?

Everything has an edge. And some edges are more perilous than others.

The edge of a dragon's temper, for example.

But we are not talking about a dragon's temper.

Not yet.

Anyone with any sense would have turned back from the edge of the forest. Even the smallest, silliest minch-wiggin stayed away from it.

But the monster kept going.

One moment, Flax was being dragged willy-nilly between trees, bushes, bracken and bark.

The next, she was flying through the air.

No, not flying.

Falling.

CHAPTER 4
Hen's Teeth and Butterfly Boots

The Queen of Hallow did not have a Dark and Terrible Secret.

She had a small, boring secret.

Probably, she thought, because *she* was small and boring.

Her name was Felicia, she was ten years old, and this was her secret: she hated being queen.

She particularly hated signing endless bits of paper before breakfast.

'This one,' said her Aunt Delilah, placing an important-looking letter on the table in front of her.

Felicia tried to read it, but Aunt Delilah's

fingers covered everything except the part where her signature was supposed to go.

'Who is it to?' asked Felicia.

'The Duke of Upsy Daisy.' Which was her aunt's way of saying, 'I'm not going to tell you.'

'What's it about?'

'Hen's teeth and butterfly boots.' Which meant, 'Mind your own business.'

Felicia didn't sigh. ('A queen does *not* sigh': Aunt Delilah)

She didn't roll her eyes. ('A queen does not roll her eyes, either.')

She just bent her head, picked up her fountain pen and signed the letter in purple ink, with lots of unnecessary flourishes.

Felicia Augustina

Alexandrina Rose Regina

She had barely finished the last flourish when Aunt Delilah whisked the letter away and put down another one.

This one looked even more important. It had a gold seal at the bottom. It was three pages long.

Aunt Delilah's hand did not quite cover the last page.

Felicia could only see a single word. But it was a word she didn't know.

'What's a Spellhound?' she asked.

Is it not strange that the Queen of Hallow did not know one of the Three Great Secrets of Hallow?

After all, every Queen and King before her knew them. Even the ones who were only ten years old.

But she didn't.

Does it make you wonder what other important things she didn't know?

Yes?

Good.

'What's a Spellhound?' asked Felicia.

Aunt Delilah's thumb came down hard, and the word vanished. 'What nonsense are you talking now? A Spellhound? There's no such thing.'

'But—' said Felicia, trying to see past her aunt's thumb.

'The word you saw was "spelunking". Now sign the letter, please, so we can get on with our duties.'

Felicia should have just signed it.

But the word had definitely been Spellhound. And that set her thinking about yesterday, when she had asked for a puppy.

Aunt Delilah had said, 'Puppies bite. We cannot have the Queen getting bitten. I will order a goldfish, instead.'

Felicia didn't want a goldfish. She wanted a puppy with a cute little nose and bright black eyes.

A puppy who would sit on her lap when she rode in the back of the royal automobile, or hide in her pocket when she was meeting the ambassador from Quill or the prime minister of Stonehuff.

A puppy who would snuggle up next to her in her big, lonely bed.

She wanted it *so much* . . .

She felt an odd sort of fizzing in her tummy.

Like a firecracker, the ones that started off slowly, so you thought they weren't going to be very interesting. But then they got *big*. And *wild*. And—

'Cake!' cried Aunt Delilah. 'The Queen needs cake!'

And almost before Felicia could draw breath, there was a whole cream cake on the table in front of her.

It had five layers, plus meringue, chocolate sprinkles and strawberries. And Cook had made it just for her.

So even though she didn't really want cake for breakfast, she ate three slices. ('A queen is *never* ungrateful.')

Then she signed the letter.

And *then* she was carried off by her ladies-in-waiting to practise being respectable, and to memorise the names of all her ancestors, right back to Bettina the Bald.

She would much rather have learnt something useful. Like, which lords and ladies had always been loyal to the throne of Hallow, and which ones had to be watched carefully.

In case they were secretly witches.

CHAPTER 5
The World Below

'Eeeeeeeeeeeeeeeeeeeeeeeeeek!' screamed Flax.

She seemed to fall forever.

Through clouds. Past startled birds. Past butter-flies and high-flying grasshoppers...

Until, with a great CRASH, the monster landed.

Flax would have hit the ground, but the monster picked itself up and kept running.

Only now they were no longer in the Floating Forest.

Now they were in the World Below, where Flax had never been. Where *no one* sensible had ever been. The World Below was where dragons came from, as well as witches, and humans.

Who would willingly go to such a place?

Flax kept her eyes shut tight, in case she saw a witch or a human. Her hands ached, but she dared not let go of the rope. She bumped, she bounced, she squeaked with terror.

And then at last, the monster began to slow down, just a little. Flax opened one eye – and realised that it wasn't a monster after all.

It was the Spellhound pup.

What's that? Yes, of course Flax knew about the Spellhounds. They are the subject of an ancient minch-wiggin rhyme.

If Spellhounds stay,
the Forest can play.
If Spellhounds leave,
the Forest must grieve.

But even without the rhyme, how could creatures so big and black and fierce stay hidden from their very curious neighbours? Especially during thunderstorms.

What have thunderstorms got to do with it?

That is such an ENORMOUS secret that I'm going to pretend you didn't ask.

When Flax recognised the monster, her fear turned to anger.

'Stop, you great lump!' she shouted. '*Stop*, you blithering idiot!'

The pup took no notice. His breath was ragged, and his ears were flat against his head. And although he slowed, he showed no sign of stopping.

So Flax began to drag herself up the rope. Hand over fist.

She nearly lost her grip several times, and had to hold on with her tail, as well as her hands and feet, while the satchel and sword bounced on her back.

But at last she reached the pup's head.

Her broken web was tangled around his nose and ears – which turned out to be a good thing, because it gave Flax something to cling to.

She clambered across it, until she was right next to the pup's left ear.

'STOP!' she shouted, in the common language of the Floating Forest.

He stopped so suddenly that she went flying, head over heels. She skidded along the ground and ended up in a heap with her whiskers crooked, the satchel on top of her, and the sheath of her sword digging into her ankle.

She groaned.

She removed the satchel and the sword.

She flicked her whiskers until they were straight.

The Spellhound pup was looking over his shoulder, and trembling from the tip of his nose to the end of his tail.

'What have you done?' snapped Flax. 'Where have you brought us? How are we going to get home again?'

The pup spun back to her. His eyes widened. 'Minch-wiggin? D-d-did you see the monster?'

Flax twitched her ears in disgust. 'The monster was you.'

'No, it was digging out our den. It growled.' The pup whimpered at the memory. 'My mother cried RUN. So I RAN.'

But— thought Flax.

But Spellhounds were ENORMOUS. Spellhounds were fierce and strong and brave. Spellhounds did that thing with thunderstorms.

What sort of creature would frighten a Spellhound?

She could think of only one.

She stood up so quickly her head spun. 'Was there a smell? A terrible scorching smell?'

'There was,' said the pup.

That was enough for Flax. 'The dragon,' she whispered. 'It must have been the dragon!'

CHAPTER 6
The Dragon

Flax's ears were pinned back in horror, and so were the pup's. Their eyes were white around the edges.

'But what would a dragon want with my parents?' whispered the pup.

'T-to eat them.'

'NooooOOOoooo!' The pup spun in a howling circle, tripped over his own feet and fell to the ground. He looked at Flax pitifully. 'Are you sure?'

'N-no.' Because who could be sure of anything about a dragon?

One of the pup's ears lifted a little. 'Then maybe it *didn't* eat them. Maybe it took them back to its den.'

'Maybe,' said Flax.

But she didn't believe it for a moment. Those Spellhounds were nothing but gnawed bones by now.

She felt sorry for the pup, but glad for herself. What if the dragon had come after minch-wiggins instead of Spellhounds?

Auntie Grub and Uncle Beech would have dragged Flax out of her cosy nest halfway up the oldest tree in Minchfold, and demanded that she defend the town and everyone in it.

And Flax would have done her best, because she loved her home.

She loved the leafy hammocks that were so nice to sleep in on hot afternoons.

And the piplum nuts, which tasted like sunshine or rain or happiness, depending on the time of day.

And the mossy-banked creek that ran right through the middle of Minchfold.

And the babies. And the grannies and grandpas. And the stories and smells and nests and swings.

And the trees themselves, which were full of magic from root to twig.

She loved it all. And if Auntie Grub and Uncle Beech had sent her to fight the dragon, she would have tried.

But there was only one possible outcome to a fight like that.

The pup blinked at her. 'You really think so? Huh? Huh?'

'Yes,' said Flax. Meaning, Yes-I-am-so-glad-the-dragon-ate-your-parents-instead-of-me.

But the pup took it completely the wrong way. He stood up. He pricked *both* his ears. 'Then they're still alive. We must go and find them.'

'What?' said Flax.

'We must find the dragon,' said the pup. 'Then we'll find my mother and father.'

And he set off in completely the wrong direction.

'Wait!' yelped Flax, running after him. 'Where are you going? Home is that way!' She pointed back the way they had come.

To her dismay, the pup didn't change direction. His tail was still tucked between his legs, and with every step he looked around nervously.

But there was something so determined about him that Flax knew he meant it.

He was going to find the dragon.

'I'll go home without you,' she squeaked.

The pup stopped and tipped his head to one side. For the first time, he seemed to look at her properly.

'You're *that* minch-wiggin. The one with the famous sword and the amazing magic.'

'Um—' said Flax.

'Destroyer-of-Dragons-and-Protector-of-her-People.' The pup's tail untucked a little. His eyes brightened. 'I'm lucky to have found you. Come on.'

And he set off again, heading north.

Flax looked up, and flinched. She looked around, and trembled.

The World Below was just *too big*. In the Floating Forest, the sky was a speckle of blue seen through the treetops. The ground was made up of tree roots and piles of fallen leaves, and little paths that wound back and forth.

Most important of all, the air sang with magic, and so did the rocks and earth and water.

But here, the sky was a wide gaping bowl that made Flax feel dizzy. There were trees, but they were few and far between. There were things that looked a bit *like* trees, except they were much too straight and only had two branches at the top, and no leaves at all.

As for the land, it was bare and flat and *dull*, as if all the magic had been drained out of it.

More than anything, Flax wanted to go home.

But she couldn't leave the pup in the World Below. What if he never came back to the Floating Forest? What if the dragon ate *him*, too?

If Spellhounds leave,

the Forest must grieve…

The rhyme made it sound as if everyone would be sad for a while, then get on with their lives.

But according to Flax's grandpa, the original rhyme didn't say 'grieve' at all. It said *griv*.

No, of course you have never heard of *griv*.

That is because you are not a minch-wiggin.

But even if you *were* a minch-wiggin, you might not know it. Hardly anyone uses the word anymore. It is too scary.

Griv means disaster. It means end-of-the-world, and hide-little-minch-wiggin-hide, and don't-*bother*-hiding-because-nothing-can-save-you.

Here are some other words you might find useful.

Perfidy, meaning lies and betrayal.

Malison, meaning a curse.

Turnkey, meaning a jailer.

Remember these words. Remember them well, so you are not taken unawares as I was, on that dreadful night when—

But no. I must tell this story in the right order.

Flax had never worried about *griv* before. The Spellhounds had shown no sign of leaving. And besides, Grandpa was always digging up old words and stories, and more than half the time they turned out to be nonsense.

But what if this one *wasn't* nonsense?

There were only three Spellhounds in the Floating Forest, and the dragon had eaten two of them.

Which left one.

Somehow, Flax had to get him back to the forest before *griv* happened.

'Wait!' she squeaked again.

And she hurried after the Spellhound pup.

CHAPTER 7
The Only Familiar Thing

The pup was pleased—

No, he didn't have a name.

Why not? Because he had not yet ████████████

████████████

And that is all I will say on the matter.

The pup was pleased to have company. He would much rather have had his parents, looming huge and powerful on either side of him. But a minch-wiggin was better than nothing.

Especially a famous minch-wiggin with a sharp sword and a satchel that bulged with magic.

He sniffed the air. Like Flax, he found the World Below too big and too flat. But the smells were AMAZING.

If his parents had been there, he would have been dashing all over the place, sticking his nose into bushes and hollows. He would have chased the wind as it swept across the grass. He would have leapt and pranced and tumbled.

But his parents had been stolen. And he was going to find them.

Beside him, Flax said, 'Well, there's no sign of the dragon. We might as well turn back.'

The pup ignored her. The ground under his paws was soft and marshy and there were plenty of puddles, so he dipped his head and drank as he walked. Flax looked around nervously, and startled at every sound.

Once, they saw a dozen whitish creatures in the distance, and he shouted to them, 'Excuse me, have you seen my parents?'

Their heads shot up, and they raced away, bleating.

'Not so loud!' hissed Flax. 'What if there are sketters about? Or mor-kits?'

'What if there are?' asked the pup.

Flax's ears flattened. 'Sketters are particularly fond of soup. *Minch-wiggin* soup. Whereas mor-kits prefer us in sandwiches.'

The pup didn't understand why someone with a satchel full of magic was worried about sketters and mor-kits.

But Flax was the only familiar thing in a very strange world. So he said, 'You can ride on my back if you like. No one has ever made Spellhound soup.'

He dropped to his haunches. Flax hesitated, looking back the way they had come, then scrambled up.

'Hold tight,' said the pup.

They crossed a stream and circled around a particularly soggy bit of ground. On the other side of it was a long black strip that ran in a straight line from east to west.

The pup lowered his head and sniffed. Heat. Strangeness. Other smells that he didn't understand.

'What is it?' asked Flax.

'I don't know,' replied the pup.

Flax slipped down from his back and touched the black strip with a cautious finger. 'It's some sort of stone.'

She put her ear to it and listened. She flinched. 'What's that sound?'

Whatever it was, it was coming closer. And the stone under the pup's paws was vibrating!

He leapt off the black strip and cowered in the grass with Flax beside him.

Just in time. Something *raced* towards them, roaring at the top of its voice. The sound grew louder and LOUDER—

And then it was past them, tearing into the distance, leaving nothing behind but an impression of two enormous eyes and a long green snout.

In the awful silence that followed when it was gone, Flax rolled onto her back, panting with terror. 'The dragon!'

What's that you say?

No, of course it wasn't a dragon.

You know that. But you are human, and have seen towns and cities.

You have seen automobiles.

If your family is very rich, you might even have ridden in one.

But imagine for a moment that you are a minchwiggin. Imagine that you have lived your whole life in the Floating Forest, where no one has even *heard* of automobiles.

Now imagine seeing and hearing, for the very first time, what Flax saw and heard.

You would call it a monster. And if your mind was already on dragons, its bonnet would be a snout. Its headlamps would be eyes.

You would be terrified.

Yes, you would. Stop arguing with me.

CHAPTER 8
A Very Strange Day

The Queen was having a very strange day.

It had begun as usual, with all those letters before breakfast, and even more letters after morning tea. Letters she wasn't allowed to read.

She glared at the space left for her signature. 'When I grow up,' she mumbled under her breath, 'I will *demand* to know what the letters say. And she will have to tell me.'

'What was that, Felicia?' Aunt Delilah handed her the fountain pen with the purple ink. 'I hope you are not complaining. A queen does *not* complain.'

'No, Aunt,' said Felicia.

But when she signed the letters, she added an extra name in protest.

Felicia Augustina

Alexandrina Dreadfullybored

Rose Regina

Aunt Delilah didn't notice.

After morning tea, however, something interesting happened.

For a start, Felicia had two new dressmakers. They were younger than her usual dressmakers, and when they were introduced—

'This is Mansie Undercroft, Your Majesty. And her cousin, Dashy Slove.'

When they were introduced, they *smiled* at her!

Not ambassadorial smiles, which were shiny and shallow. Or prime ministerial smiles, which were oily and overbearing.

Proper smiles, as if Felicia was a real person and they were prepared to like her.

Felicia didn't smile back. ('A queen does *not* smile at servants.') But she blinked in a friendly fashion and hoped they would understand what she meant.

And then—

And then, when Aunt Delilah had been called away to deal with something important, and the two dressmakers were pinning up the hem of Felicia's new dress, and Felicia was trying to stand still but finding it awfully hard because they were so nice, and she wasn't used to people being nice—

'We're both awfully sorry about your parents, Your Majesty,' murmured Dashy.

Felicia froze.

No one talked to her about her parents. Not ever. The only reason she knew what they looked like was the gold-framed painting behind the throne.

Her mother, Queen Alyss, had red hair like Felicia's, and a determined smile. She wore a small crown of white gold, and looked straight ahead,

so that when Felicia stood in front of the painting, she felt as if her mother was smiling right at her.

Her father, Prince Malik, gazed into the distance with his hand on his hip and one foot forward. He had black hair and a pointed black beard, and he looked very noble.

They both wore ermine robes and carried swords.

No one had ever told Felicia what had happened to them. Just that they had died when she was six months old, which made her the Queen, no matter how much she hated it.

'Fancy a dragon coming right into the middle of Hallow to steal the Queen and Prince Malik,' said Mansie, shaking her head. 'What a terrible thing.'

Felicia opened her mouth to say, 'What dragon? What are you *talking* about?'

But before she could utter a single word, Aunt Delilah reappeared. She grabbed Felicia's arm and marched her away, saying, 'It is time for your deportment lesson, Your Majesty.'

Aunt Delilah walked *very* fast when she was cross. 'Deportment was yesterday,' gasped Felicia as they bustled past the schoolroom.

'So it was,' said her aunt, without slowing down. 'Never mind. You need the practice.'

She pushed Felicia into the royal bedchamber. 'I will return in half an hour. Use the back straightener. I expect to see *grace*, Your Majesty. Grace and dignity.'

Then she slammed the door and left Felicia alone, with her hem half up and half down, and her mind a-whirl with questions.

CHAPTER 9
We're Going Home

The dragon was far worse than anything Flax had imagined.

It was bigger.

It was noisier.

It had passed so close that it was a wonder it hadn't seen them, and snatched them up and eaten them.

'We're going home,' she declared, as soon as she got her breath back. 'We're going home right now.'

She turned away from the black stone, and began to hurry south across the flat, marshy land, sure the pup would follow.

But he didn't. He stared towards the east, where the dragon had gone, and made a frightened noise in his throat.

Then he set off after it!

Flax couldn't believe her eyes. 'It'll eat you!' she shouted, as the pup got further and further away. 'It'll snatch you up and gnaw your bones.'

The pup looked over his shoulder.

'And then,' shouted Flax, 'there won't be a single Spellhound left in the Floating Forest!'

To her relief, that brought him trotting back.

'It's dreadful about your parents,' she said when he stood in front of her. 'But it's no use throwing your life after theirs. You don't want to mess with that dragon – what a horrible great thing it was. Did you see its snout, and those awful eyes—'

Flax knew she was babbling, but she didn't care. She was giddy with gladness, because they were going home, where the only things she had to worry about were sketters and mor-kits.

(And the Dark and Terrible Secret, of course.

But right now, even that didn't seem quite so bad.)

The pup gazed down at her. 'I don't want it to eat me.'

'Of course you don't,' said Flax. 'No one wants to be eaten by a dragon. Now let's go before it comes back.'

'I don't want it to eat you, either.'

'Which is why we're going to hurry,' said Flax, turning south again.

The pup didn't move. 'You could use your amazing magic to hide us. If the dragon can't see us or hear us or smell us, it won't eat us.'

'But we're not going after the dragon.'

'Yup, we are.'

'No, we're *not*.'

'*I* am,' said the pup.

Flax's heart bumped in her chest. She stared southward, wondering if the cloud on the horizon was the Floating Forest.

Maybe. Maybe not. But she had no doubt she could find it.

Why was she so sure?

Because minch-wiggins are famous for their sense of direction. You could blindfold a minch-wiggin, spin her around seven times, tip her upside down and toss her into the deepest, darkest well you could find, and she would still be able to tell you which direction was north, and which was south and west and east.

If, that is, she was willing to talk to you after you had treated her so badly.

Flax trotted in a small circle. It helped her think.

Then she trotted in a bigger circle. Round and round, while the pup watched.

'If I go home without him,' she mumbled to herself, '*griv* might come. Because Grandpa might have been wrong some of the time. But he was right some of the time, too.'

She wondered if it would come straight away. Or if it would hold off for a while.

'Maybe if I try really hard to keep the pup safe, and to get him back to the forest as soon as possible, *griv* will leave us alone.'

She stopped halfway around the circle. It wasn't a very good plan. She didn't know *how* she was going to keep the pup safe, or how she was going to get him back to the forest if he didn't want to go.

But at least it gave her a glimmer of hope.

She wrapped her arms around the satchel. 'I'm not supposed to use the magic for small things,' she said to the pup. 'It's only for destroying dragons.'

'But you know how it works?'

Flax *did* know how it worked. No one had told her – it had just sort of popped into her head after Grandpa died.

She nodded. It was a very small, uncertain nod, and the answering wag of the pup's tail was a very small, uncertain wag.

'Please?' he said. 'Please, Flax?'

CHAPTER 10
A Thread of Magic

Flax unbuckled the satchel and reached inside.

Her fingers closed over a thread of wild magic.

She held it carefully so it couldn't escape, and drew it out of the satchel.

She tied three knots, one at each end of the thread and one in the middle.

It sounds easy, doesn't it? You are probably thinking that *you* could work magic, too, if only you had the right sort of thread.

After all, most people can tie knots.

But human fingers are far too big for such delicate work. And besides, these weren't just any old knots.

The first knot Flax tied was so small that not even she could see it.

And minch-wiggins have very good eyesight.

The second knot was so quiet that not even she could hear it.

And minch-wiggins have AMAZING ears.

The third knot was the hardest. Flax started it one way, then changed her mind halfway through.

She mumbled, 'Um—' and, 'I don't know whether—' and, 'Maybe if—'

She undid it and tried again. But this time she held her breath until she was done.

'I think I've got it,' she muttered. 'Pup, can you smell this knot?'

The pup sniffed the thread. 'Nope. Nothing.'

'Good,' said Flax.

She put her hand on the pup's shoulder, so the magic would affect him, too. And she swallowed the thread.

The pup watched her anxiously. 'Did it work?'

'I...don't know.' Flax had expected something big and dramatic. But nothing had changed – except for her nose, which was suddenly dreadfully itchy.

'I can still see us,' said the pup.

'So can I.'

'We'd better test it, huh?' The pup raised his head and sniffed the air. 'There's some people over that way. Let's try it out on them.'

The people-over-that-way turned out to be the same sort of bleating creatures that had run from Flax and the pup earlier. They were crowded under a tree with a lumpy trunk and twisted branches.

Standing in front of them was an entirely different sort of creature.

'Is that a *giant minch-wiggin*?' whispered the pup, crouching in the long grass with Flax on his back.

Flax blinked. The creature walked on two legs like a minch-wiggin. And it had hands like a minch-wiggin, instead of paws or hoofs.

But it was much too big, its ears were the wrong shape, and it didn't have whiskers or a black-tipped tail.

'I think,' she whispered, 'it might be a human.'

She tried to remember Grandpa's stories about humans.

They were big, that was the main thing.

And not very clever.

Or was that trolls?

The pup crept towards the tree, ready to turn and run if he and Flax were seen. But the bleating creatures ignored them.

So did the human.

'*Burble,*' it said. '*Gomp. Skirleen. Squawkeen. Miffteen—*'

'What's it doing?' whispered the pup.

'Counting, I think.'

'I wonder if it can hear us. Hello? HELLOOO?'

'Shhhhhh!' hissed Flax.

But the human didn't even turn its head. '*Mempty-dun,*' it counted. '*Mempty-boo. Mempty-zee—*'

The pup crept out of the grass with Flax clinging to the scruff of his neck. He sniffed the human's legs. He sneezed.

'Shhhhhhh!' said Flax again.

'*Derpty,*' said the human. '*Derpty-dun. Derpty-boo—*'

'It's all right, it can't see us,' cried the pup. 'It can't

hear us or smell us! Your magic is AMAZING, Flax! Now we can get my parents back!'

And with Flax still clutching his neck, he galloped away from the human and after the dragon.

CHAPTER 11
Nothing Interesting
Happened

For the next few days, nothing interesting happened. Not to Flax and the pup and not to the Queen.

What's that? You want details?

Very well.

Flax and the pup walked beside the black stone.

They argued about whether they should turn back or not.

They both whimpered in their sleep and hoped the other one didn't hear them.

On the third day, they left the flat land behind and climbed into low-lying hills, where the tree branches were even more twisted, and grey rock poked up through the grass.

They found seeds to eat, and roots and milk thistles, and they drank from the streams that crossed under the black stone. They saw bleating creatures in the distance, and several humans, but didn't go anywhere near them.

They walked some more.

They argued some more.

They whimpered in their sleep...

As for the Queen, she signed letters.

And more letters.

She practised her deportment.

She ate cake.

She sat on an uncomfortable chair and listened to the ambassador from Quill talking about trade for *two hours*.

She tried not to wriggle. ('A queen does not wriggle.')

She tried not to complain. ('A queen does *not* complain.')

She signed *more* letters...

Have you had enough yet?

Of course you have. This is a *story*, which means we leave out the boring bits.

The only thing you really need to know is that Flax and the pup saw more dragons, rushing up and down the black strip.

Some of them were red. Some were silver or green. Some went east, some went west.

There were so many of them, and the whole thing was so strange and frightening, that on the fifth day Flax sat on the grass with her head in her hands and wept.

But then she stood up again and kept going. Because what else could she do?

On the seventh day, they came to a town.

The town, though they didn't yet know it.

The town of High Kinnik, where the royal palace of Hallow can be found, surrounded by the royal park.

CHAPTER 12
The Human Town

The human town was nothing at all like minchwiggin towns. There were no nests or vines or hammocks. There were no minch-wiggin babies scurrying along the branches of ancient trees, or minch-wiggin grandmothers huddled over a game of Sniksnak, with dice in their hands and tiles hidden up their sleeves.

The human town was made of grey stone buildings and grey stone streets. It was smelly and noisy, and a hundred times bigger than Minchfold, where Flax lived.

No, a thousand times bigger. And *ten* thousand times more frightening.

There were dragons everywhere. They roared past Flax and the pup, puffing smoke and howling around corners.

There were hounds, too, of all shapes and sizes, though none as big as a Spellhound.

There were birds (not many), and mice (a lot). There were earwigs and cockroaches and spiders.

And there were humans, who looked like giant minch-wiggins (except for the ears, tail and whiskers).

Flax knew they couldn't see her. She knew they couldn't hear her or smell her.

But still she trembled and flinched and folded her ears, trying to keep out the noise. And she longed for the soft, winding paths of the Floating Forest, and the quiet green leaves above her.

So when she saw a tree standing in the middle of a grey stone street, she ran towards it, with the pup loping beside her.

It wasn't a piplum, a droopy oak, or a spider-nut tree. Its leaves were a strange shape, and its acorns were small.

But it was still a tree.

Flax pressed her ear to the bark and listened for the deep, slow song that only a minch-wiggin can hear.

It wasn't there. Unlike the trees of the Floating Forest (which were filled with magic from root to twig) *this* tree had no song at all.

Flax's heart fell. No wonder the World Below seemed so dull and strange. The trees were alive, but not in the same way. They didn't sing. They didn't speak. They didn't even hum.

She sighed, and peeled one of the acorns. 'Pup, does this smell all right to you?'

The pup swallowed something dead he had found on the other side of the tree, and dipped his nose into the palm of Flax's hand.

'Yup.' His big red tongue looped around the acorn and carried it to his mouth.

Flax peeled another one.

She nibbled on it carefully at first. But it tasted almost like the acorns from the Floating Forest, so before long both she and the pup were eating them as fast as they could.

When they were no longer quite so hungry, they sat beneath the tree and watched the dragons race past.

'How are we going to find the right one?' asked the pup.

'I don't see how we can,' said Flax. 'They all look the same. They all *sound* the same.'

She peeped at the pup out of the corner of her eye. 'I guess it's time to give up and go home.

Won't it be wonderful to see the Floating Forest again?'

The pup ignored her. 'The first one we met was green, so . . .'

Three green dragons roared past.

The pup's ears drooped. 'We need to know what they're saying. Then we might be able to find the right one.'

Flax didn't want to know what the dragons were saying. It was probably something terrifying.

In one of Grandpa's stories, the dragon stalked through the Floating Forest, reciting:

Fat or thin,

Small or big 'un,

I. Smell. Minch. Wiggin.

No, it is not a very good rhyme. But you don't need to be good at rhymes when you weigh half a tonne and can breathe fire.

I mean, would *you* walk up to a dragon and say, 'Excuse me, that was really dreadful'?

Before you answer, please note that dragons do not take kindly to literary criticism.

CHAPTER 13
What are the Dragons Saying?

'I. Smell. Minch. Wiggin,' whispered Flax, and a shiver ran from the tip of her whiskers right down to her toes.

But after seven days of travelling together, she knew how stubborn the pup was.

She picked up her satchel and undid the buckle.

The pup sat up, ears pricked. 'You're going to use your magic again?'

'I'm going to try,' said Flax.

She picked out a thread.

Put it back.

Picked out a bigger one.

Stared at it.

The *can't-see-me* knot had been obvious. So had the *can't-hear-me*. The *can't-smell-me* had been harder, though she'd worked it out in the end.

But how was she supposed to tie an *understand-what-they're-saying* knot? And what if she got it wrong? She would have wasted a whole thread.

Maybe if she tied a knot that looked like a mouth...

No, that didn't feel right.

What if she made it look like an ear?

But that wasn't right, either.

Perhaps if she made it look like a mouth *and* an ear...

The pup's big black nose nudged her hands. 'Is it done yet?' he asked, in the common language of the Floating Forest.

'Not yet,' said Flax, in the same tongue. 'I don't know how— Maybe if I *talk* to it—'

In the end, she tied a perfectly ordinary knot. But as her fingers twisted the thread into a loop, and slipped one end past the other, she whispered to it in the common language of the Floating Forest.

Kept whispering as she rested her hand on the pup's shoulder.

Swallowed the thread...

The sounds of the town changed. And suddenly, Flax could understand every word the humans were saying.

She heard, 'Come along, Pinch, don't dawdle!'

And, 'Fresh figs, all the way from Quill!'

And, 'Did you hear about the witch they caught, out near Mount Tangle? Oh yes, she was definitely a witch. She looked just like anyone else, but she had feathers on her elbows and no heartbeat at all – that's how you can tell.'

Flax could understand the hounds, too.

She heard, 'Whoa, dead rat. This is my lucky day!'

And, 'Wanna go for a run? Huh? Huh?'

And, 'Do I want a biscuit? Of *course* I want a biscuit!'

She could understand the mice and the earwigs and the birds nesting in the eaves, and the spiders and caterpillars.

But she couldn't understand the dragons.

They just roared. There was no sense to the sound. There were no words.

Flax wondered if the thread of magic had been too small. Maybe dragon language was so big and important that you needed a big, important thread to understand it.

Or maybe she'd got the knot wrong.

But before she could work out what to do, one of the dragons stopped nearby.

A door opened in its side. A human climbed out and walked away, unharmed.

Flax and the pup stared at each other in astonishment. 'The dragon – ate the human?' the pup said uncertainly. 'But it – escaped?'

'Through a *door*?' said Flax. 'I've never heard of dragons having a door in their side.'

She studied the monster. 'I think it's asleep.

And – and even if it wakes up, it can't see us. Or hear us. Or smell us.'

Before she could lose her courage, she stood up and crept towards the sleeping dragon, with the pup padding beside her.

There wasn't just a door in the dragon's side. There was a window.

The pup sniffed the long snout. 'It doesn't smell like the dragon that stole my parents.'

'I don't think it's a dragon at all,' whispered Flax, peeping through the window. 'I don't think it's even alive.'

She expected the pup to be pleased. *She* was pleased, and not quite as frightened as she had been a few minutes ago.

But the pup sat on his haunches and let out a howl of anguish. 'Then where's the dragon? Where are my mother and father? What if I never see them again? What if I never find them?'

And he fell to the ground in a heap of long legs and misery.

CHAPTER 14
A Small Forest

When night fell, Flax and the pup left the tree behind and went looking for somewhere safe to sleep.

But nothing about this town felt safe.

Not until they found the stone wall.

On the other side of it were hundreds of trees. Flax could smell their leaves. She could hear their branches, rustling in the night breeze.

It almost sounded like home.

But when she scrambled up the wall, taking care not to let the sheath of her sword bang against the stone, it didn't *look* like home.

The trees were set in neat rows, instead of

growing in wild confusion. There was no soft green moss for lining nests, and no thorny undergrowth for hiding from mor-kits. No fallen branches for sitting on while the grandpas told stories, no rotting logs, no beetles or ants or horned globs. And in the middle of it was a human building, ten times as grand and important-looking as any Flax had seen so far.

But she didn't care about buildings. Not when there were trees (even though they were nowhere near as nice as the trees of the Floating Forest).

She slid down the far side of the wall and dashed across the grass. She heard a thump behind her, and she and the pup reached the shelter of the trees at the same time.

There they stayed.

In a small forest, which was good.

With no idea what to do next.

Which was bad.

Meanwhile, Felicia was lying in her big, lonely bed, with the covers pulled up to her chin.

The gold crowns embroidered on her royal nightdress scratched her arms.

The gold hairpins, set in her royal hair every night to hold it in place, scratched her scalp.

Moonlight filtered through the windows, and shone on a brand-new fish tank, which sat on top of the royal chest of drawers.

'Why won't anyone talk to me about my parents?' Felicia whispered to the fish. 'Why didn't they tell me about the dragon?'

The fish glared at her. Its little mouth opened and shut, as if to say, 'A queen does *not* ask questions.'

'I can't help it,' whispered Felicia. 'I want to know the answers.'

But the fish kept glaring. So Felicia crept out of bed, picked up her dress from the chair where her ladies-in-waiting had left it, and draped it over the tank.

Then she knelt in front of the royal wardrobe, opened the secret drawer at the bottom, and reached into the back corner.

Her fingers closed around an ancient pair of pyjama pants. She took them out and pressed them to her cheek.

The pyjama pants had crowns embroidered on them, too. But they were so old that most of the gold thread had worn away, and now they were soft and comforting.

Extra comforting because they used to belong to Felicia's mother, Queen Alyss.

Extra *extra* comforting, because no one except Felicia knew she had found them in a pile of polishing rags and sneaked them up to her bedchamber.

She took off her scratchy nightdress and pulled on the pyjama pants. They were too big, so she rolled up the legs and tied a ribbon around her waist to keep them from falling down.

Then she sat on the floor (which queens were *not*

supposed to do), and whispered, 'What happened to you, Mother? Were you and Father really taken by a dragon?'

She wished she could ask Mansie Undercroft or Dashy Slove, the new dressmakers. But they had disappeared the same day they arrived, while Felicia was walking up and down her bedchamber with *The History of Hallow in Five Volumes* balanced on her head.

You are probably thinking that even one disappearing dressmaker is strange. Two is even stranger.

But any number of things had disappeared from the palace in the years since Felicia was born.

Her parents.

Her nursemaid.

Her Uncle Edwin, who was Regent for a year and a half after her parents died.

A book about dragons that Felicia had found on a forgotten shelf of the palace library. (A book much older than all the *other* books about dragons.)

A tapestry with an enormous black dog in the bottom left-hand corner.

Laughter.

Love.

Happiness...

You get the idea. The royal palace of Hallow was not the sort of place where you should take your eye off anything you valued.

Because when you looked again, it might not be there.

'Family emergency,' Aunt Delilah had said, when Felicia asked her about Mansie and Dashy. 'No, they will not be coming back. Why not? A queen does not ask pointless questions, Your Majesty. And a queen does *not* sulk.'

'I wasn't sulking,' Felicia whispered now. 'I was wondering.'

She stroked the worn material that covered her knees. She hugged herself, and wished there was someone she could talk to. Someone who would understand how lonely she was.

Someone who would tell her the truth.

CHAPTER 15
We Have to Keep Searching

'Maybe your parents have gone back to the Floating Forest,' Flax said to the pup. 'Maybe they climbed out a door in the dragon's side and escaped. Maybe they're in the den, right now, wondering where you are.'

The pup looked at her pitifully. 'Dragons don't have doors in their sides. You said so yourself.'

'Yes, but maybe—'

'We have to keep searching.'

'But where?' said Flax.

'I don't know. I don't knoooOOOOOoooow!'

'Hush, not so loud!' Flax's nose itched, which meant the *can't-see-us-can't-hear-us-can't-smell-us* magic was still working. But it was best to be cautious.

The pup's howl subsided to a wordless whimper. Flax put her head in her hands and wondered how on earth she was going to get him back to the Floating Forest.

Have you ever heard a dog howl with sadness and loneliness?

It is a heartbreaking sound, is it not?

Now take that sound and double it.

Triple it.

Quadruple it.

The howl of a Spellhound pup is like nothing else on earth. If you wish to pause for a moment and weep, I can be persuaded to wait.

But not for long. We are at a *crux*. A vital moment. A point where two halves of the story might come together – or might not.

So wipe your eyes and pay attention.

The moonlight slid off the dress covering the fish tank and touched Felicia's toes. In the royal park outside her window, something howled.

'OoooooooooooOOOOOOOOOooooooooo!'

It was such a desolate sound that Felicia scrambled to her feet and poked her head out the open window.

The howl turned to a whimper.

'It's a dog,' whispered Felicia. 'A puppy. What's it doing in the royal park? It must be lost.'

She imagined a puppy with sorrowful eyes crying for its mother.

She swallowed. 'A queen is *not* disobedient,' she reminded herself.

But surely a queen should be allowed to have a puppy? Even if it was just for one night?

It would disappear in the morning, of course,

just as the tapestry and the dragon book and the dressmakers had disappeared.

But morning was hours away...

Felicia felt a fizz of excitement in her tummy, and automatically pushed it down. But a tiny bit of it crept back again. Enough to make her feel brave. And rebellious.

She took her oldest shoes from the secret drawer (the ones she wasn't allowed to wear).

She took her oldest coat (which Aunt Delilah thought she had thrown away).

She removed the gold hairpins and tied her hair back with another ribbon.

Then she checked her pocket for her emergency supply of green jellybabies, slung her leg over the windowsill, and clambered out.

CHAPTER 16
A Human Girl

'Are you sure we can't go home?' asked Flax.

The pup whimpered again.

But then he stopped whimpering and sat up. He stared towards the building. He sniffed the air.

'There's a human,' he whispered to Flax, 'coming this way.'

Flax put her ear to the ground and heard footsteps. 'They won't be able to see us or hear us or smell us. We'll just stay here until they go past.'

But she drew her sword, just in case. Then she and the pup stood close to the tree trunk, and waited.

'There,' whispered the pup.

A shadowy figure crept between the trees. It seemed to be searching for something.

Not us, Flax reminded herself. *Can't-see-us. Can't-hear-us. Can't-smell-us.*

The figure came closer. It was a human girl, and she was calling softly, 'Where are you? Don't be afraid. I want to help.'

What was she searching for? A bird? Another human?

She's going to walk straight past us, thought Flax. *She won't even know we're here.*

But the human didn't walk past.

She stopped. She stared at the pup. 'Oh, you're *much* bigger than I expected.'

'Who's she talking to?' whispered Flax.

'Me, I think,' said the pup.

'You can talk,' said the human, clasping her hands in front of her. 'A talking dog. A *huge* talking dog!'

'I'm not a dog,' said the pup. 'I'm a Spe—'

'Hush!' cried Flax, leaping forward. 'Don't say it.'

The human bent down to take a closer look at Flax. 'A pixie? With a sword? A talking dog and a *pixie with a sword*! Except you've got whiskers. And a tail. I didn't know pixies had whiskers and tails.'

Flax and the pup looked at each other. 'She can definitely see us,' said the pup.

'Of course I can see you,' said the human. 'Though I've never seen anything *like* you.'

Flax couldn't understand how this human could see them when none of the others had been able to.

Unless...

She clutched her sword. She tried to look tall and dangerous (which isn't easy for a minch-wiggin). 'Are you—' Her voice cracked. 'Are you a w-w-witch?'

The pup rolled his eyes in horror. 'A *witch?* NoooooOOOooooo! We've fallen into the hands of a *witch!*'

You may be wondering why Flax and the pup were so scared. After all, the witches *you* know are probably nice old women who live in forest clearings with their cats, and use their powers to help people.

They get rid of warts and cure the mumbling sickness. They find lost wedding rings, lost sheep and lost children.

The witches of Hallow are not like that.

The witches of Hallow work in the shadows where no one can see them. They gather on the edge of darkness. They have feathers on their elbows, and silence where their heartbeats should be.

The witches of Hallow do not concern themselves with lost children. Not unless they are making the invisibility potion, which requires '*three fyngers of small childe*'.

Then they will search harder than anyone.

CHAPTER 17
I'm Not a Witch

'No, I'm not a witch!' cried the human girl. 'I'm the Qu—' She stopped.

'The what?' demanded Flax.

The girl looked over her shoulder at the building. She looked back at Flax and the pup. She bit her lip. 'I'm the qu— the quite ordinary fourth chambermaid.'

Flax decided to believe her, because the day had been long and frightening, and she didn't think she could deal with a witch right now.

(Or ever, to be honest.)

But the sooner we get away from here, the better, she thought. *We've got enough problems without getting mixed up with humans. They're not as bad as witches or dragons or griv. But they're still trouble.*

She sheathed the sword and picked up her satchel. 'Nice to meet you, quite ordinary fourth chambermaid—'

'My name is F— er – Rose.'

'Feroze?' said the pup.

'No. Just Rose.'

Flax put on a polite smile. 'Nice to meet you, Rose. But we must be—'

'What's a Spe—?' asked the human.

'Nothing,' Flax said quickly. She definitely wasn't going to tell the human about Spellhounds. Even if she wasn't a witch. 'I mean – um – it's a *special* dog. But only because he's so big. And he can talk. Apart from that, he's completely ordinary, aren't you, pup?'

'I am?' The pup tipped his head to one side.

'You are,' said Flax. 'Now, we must go.'

'But where did you come from?' asked Rose.

The pup, who was much too trusting, wagged his tail. 'We come from the F—'

'The Far Away,' interrupted Flax. 'The *Far*, Far Away. Too far for you to bother with. And it's a completely boring place, no one ever wants to go there. Now, if you'll excuse us, we must—'

'Why did you come here?' asked Rose.

And before Flax could think of an answer, the pup blurted, 'The dragon.'

Rose's eyes widened. 'What dragon?'

'It stole my parents,' said the pup. 'We're going to find them and get them back.'

Rose put her hand over her mouth. 'The dragon stole my parents, too! I – I want to go with you!'

CHAPTER 18
A Door

Felicia didn't really mean it. She was the Queen, after all. She couldn't just run off with a pixie and a giant dog in the middle of the night.

All the same, the words seemed to hang in the air in front of her.

As if she *had* meant it.

As if it was a real possibility...

But it wasn't.

It definitely wasn't.

For a start, Aunt Delilah would be furious if Felicia disappeared. She'd stomp up and down the corridors of the palace, shouting at people. She'd narrow her eyes and blame the ladies-in-waiting and the guards and anyone else who crossed her path.

But I wouldn't be here to see it, thought Felicia.

The fizzing in her tummy was back. It felt like a window. Or maybe a door, where she hadn't even known there was one.

And it was ajar. Just the tiniest little bit...

If I find the dragon, I might learn what happened to my parents, she thought. *It's the sort of thing a queen should know.*

She looked at the pixie, who only came up to her knee. She looked at the dog, who was pitch-black and enormous, with ears like black flags and paws as big as the royal dinner plates (the special ones that were only used at banquets).

'I want to go with you,' she said again.

And this time she meant it.

The pixie shook her head. 'Definitely not.'

'Three might be better than two, Flax,' said the dog. 'Don't you think? Huh? Huh?'

'No,' said the pixie.

'But I could help,' said Felicia. 'I'm good at—'

What *was* she good at? Signing official letters she wasn't allowed to read. Walking around her bedchamber with *The History of Hallow in Five Volumes* on her head. Smiling at ambassadors and prime ministers when she was tired and bored.

None of those things seemed likely to change the pixie's mind.

But perhaps—

'If you're from far, far away,' she said, 'you probably don't know much about Hallow.'

The pixie crossed her arms. 'We know enough.'

'We don't, Flax,' said the dog (who looked awfully like the big black dog on the tapestry that had disappeared).

'We *do*,' snapped Flax.

'But I know heaps of things,' Felicia said desperately. 'I know how many bales of wool we produce every year, and where the stone is mined for public buildings, and where the best grapes grow for wine...'

She stopped. Even to her, it did not sound like a useful list.

'Can you fight a dragon?' demanded Flax.

'I – I don't think so,' Felicia said in a small voice.

'Then you're no use to us. Not unless the dragon asks for grapes, or stone. Which isn't very likely.'

Felicia's shoulders drooped. Of course they didn't want her. No one wanted her, not for anything important or useful.

Even when the ambassadors and prime ministers pretended to smile at her, they were really smiling at Aunt Delilah. She held the power in Hallow. She wrote the letters that Felicia signed. She made the decisions.

With a sigh, Felicia turned back towards the palace. Tonight had been more interesting than the past hundred days put together. And for a moment, she had thought her life might change.

But it hadn't.

And it wouldn't.

'Goodbye then,' she said over her shoulder.

At least she could still be polite. 'Good luck with the dragon.'

Behind her, the giant dog was arguing with the pixie.

'No,' said the pixie. 'No no no!'

'Yup,' said the dog. 'Otherwise we'll never *mumble mumble mumble.*'

A tiny leaf of hope sprouted in Felicia's heart.

She half turned, just as the dog raised his voice and said, 'I don't suppose you know where the dragon lives?'

CHAPTER 19
Did You Smell a Terrible Smell?

Flax stomped between the neat rows of trees, staring straight ahead.

Behind her, Rose and the pup were telling each other the-dragon-stole-my-parents stories.

'Did you smell a terrible smell?' asked the pup.

'I don't remember,' said Rose. 'I was very small when it happened.'

'*I* smelled a terrible smell. And my mother shouted RUN, so I ran.' The pup's voice sank to an almost-whisper. 'Dragons are *very* powerful. Only a dragon could overcome a Spe—'

'A special dog,' snapped Flax. 'Who talks far too much.'

She glared over her shoulder at the pup, who was hopeless at keeping secrets.

She glared even harder at Rose. 'There's no need for you to come with us. You could just tell us where the dragon lives. And if your parents are there, which they won't be, we could – um – come back and let you know. Or – or set them free. So *they* could come back.'

The truth was, Flax didn't *want* to know where the dragon lived. If they didn't know, they couldn't go after it. And then the pup would have to agree to go home.

He'd be sad, of course. But his parents were dead, Flax was sure of it. Which meant there was only one sensible thing to do.

Get back to the Floating Forest as quickly as possible.

Griv, she thought. *I have to save the forest from griv.*

'Can we go a little faster?' asked Rose. 'If they miss me, they might come after me.'

Flax stopped. 'I thought you weren't important.'

'I'm not.'

'Then why would they come after you?'

'Because – because there'll be no one to empty the chamberpots.'

'What's a chamberpot?' asked Flax.

Rose told her.

'Ewwwww,' said Flax.

But she sped up, because it was bad enough having one human with them without being chased by a dozen more with smelly chamberpots.

When they came to the wall, Flax scrambled to the top and down the other side. The pup leapt over it, just as he had done earlier in the night.

They set off again.

Behind them, a plaintive voice said, 'Wait for me?'

Flax rolled her eyes and went back to the wall. 'Hurry up,' she hissed through the stone. 'We want to be well away from here before morning.'

'How do you climb it?' called Rose. 'Qu—

quite ordinary fourth chambermaids don't get much practice at climbing.'

Flax would have left her there. But the pup bounded back over the wall, and Flax could hear him pushing and encouraging.

'No, I can't reach it,' said Rose. 'I definitely can't. Is there another way? Ow, you didn't have to nip me! Yes, I think I *can* reach it, after all—'

At last, the human girl scrambled to the top of the wall. 'How do I get down?' she asked.

Flax rested her head against the stone and sighed.

Minch-wiggins are almost as good at climbing as they are at finding their way home.

Which is not surprising, given their towns are built in trees, and their babies learn to swing from the branches before they can walk.

Queens, generally speaking, are *not* good at climbing. They might be able to scramble out a ground-floor window without too much trouble. But that is very different from climbing a wall.

Or a tree.

Or a mountain.

If, however, you need someone to tell a convincing lie, a queen will do a much better job than a minch-wiggin.

Is this important?

In a good story, *everything* is important.

CHAPTER 20
A Rich, Happy Country

According to the map on the first page of the very old book that had disappeared from the palace library, the dragon lived in the labyrinth at Mount Tangle.

Felicia had never been to Mount Tangle—

No, *Rose* had never been to Mount Tangle.

A girl called Felicia would not run away in the middle of the night with a giant dog and a pixie.

But Rose would.

'That's who I am now,' she said under her breath. 'I'm Rose, and I mustn't forget it.'

Rose had hardly ever been outside the palace, except to drive around High Kinnick in the back of the royal automobile, with Aunt Delilah beside her saying, 'Look more regal, child. No, not like that. Lift your chin. *Not* like that; you look as if you're about to fall over backwards. Now wave to your subjects. Good heavens, anyone would think you were trying to clean the window. A queen does *not* clean windows. Wave *regally*.'

As a result, everything she saw that night was new to her.

The royal automobile had never gone down *this* street, with its tumbledown houses and leaky roofs.

It had never driven past these ragged children, asleep in the gutter. Or the one-legged soldier. Or the old woman with trembling hands and weepy eyes.

Felic— No. *Rose* had been taught that Hallow was a rich, happy country. She had believed that everyone ate as well as she did.

(Perhaps not *quite* as well. She was the Queen, after all.)

Now, she saw a very small part of the truth.

She wanted to wake the children and say, 'I'm sorry, but I didn't know.'

She wanted to take off her coat, which was far better than anything the old woman wore, and give it to her.

But if she spoke to them, they might recognise her from her picture on the stamps and coins. And they'd be sure to tell someone, who would tell someone else, who would tell someone *else*. And somehow, word would get to Aunt Delilah, even though it was the middle of the night.

And then Rose would have to go back to being Queen. She'd have to spend her mornings signing letters she wasn't allowed to read, and her afternoons balancing books on her head and smiling at visiting ambassadors.

And she'd never learn the truth about her parents.

So she didn't stop. Instead, as she hurried down the awful streets, she whispered, 'Sorry. Sorry.

I'll come back when I've found out what happened to my mother and father. I'll come back and – and *do* something.'

Maybe next time she was in the royal automobile, she would say, 'Excuse me, Aunt Delilah, could we go that way for a change?'

And then Aunt Delilah would see the broken windows and the tumbledown roofs and be just as horrified as Rose was.

And between them they could work out a scheme to make sure people got better clothes, more food, and better houses.

Rose tried to imagine it.

But she couldn't. Aunt Delilah would say, 'Go that way? Ridiculous. Be quiet, child, and wave. No, not like that. Wave *properly.*'

For the first time in her life, Rose found herself wondering whether her aunt was a *good* Regent.

And what on earth Rose could do about it if she wasn't.

CHAPTER 21
A Plan

By the time they came to the outskirts of town, Flax had a plan.

'The dragon lives north of here?' she asked.

It was still night-time, and the empty road stretched ahead of them, with hedges on either side. The few remaining houses were in darkness. The moon was sinking slowly in the west.

'Yes,' said Rose.

'How do we get there?'

'We follow this road until it crosses the Darting River. And then we – um – actually, it's a bit complicated. I'll have to show you.'

Flax didn't believe for a moment that it was

complicated. Rose was just making sure they didn't leave her behind.

'The road doesn't go directly north,' she said, squinting at the black stone.

'No, I think it winds a bit,' said Rose.

'We haven't got time for winding roads,' said Flax. 'We'll go across country and get there quicker.'

The pup wagged his tail and bounced a couple of times. 'Quicker is good.'

But Rose said, 'What if we get lost?'

'Flax won't get lost,' said the pup. 'Minch-wiggins are famous for their sense of direction.'

'Minch-wiggins? What's a minch-wiggin?'

'Just another name for pixies,' Flax said firmly. 'Now, are you coming?'

She climbed through a gap in the fence and set off at a very slight angle to the road. She wriggled under a hedge, then made her way through long grass and past a dark house, with Rose and the pup following her.

At first, she went directly north. But before long, she veered a little bit to one side.

Rose and the pup were too busy bombarding each other with questions to notice.

'What was that?' asked the pup, looking back towards the road.

'An automobile,' said Rose.

'Not a dragon?'

'No, automobiles are nothing like dragons. Why didn't those people in town stare at you?'

'They couldn't see us,' said the pup.

Flax veered a bit more. Ahead of them, sleepy

white shapes loomed out of the darkness.

'What are they?' asked the pup.

'Sheep. *Why* couldn't those people see you?'

'Because of the mag—'

'Because they couldn't see very well in the dark,' interrupted Flax.

'But I can see you perfectly well,' said Rose.

Which is strange, thought Flax. *I don't understand it. I don't like it.*

Another hedge. Another fence. Another house. Flax veered a bit more...and a bit more...and a bit more...until they were going due east instead of north.

By then, they were all yawning. So when they came to a clump of trees and hedges with no houses nearby, Flax stopped and said, 'We should get some sleep.'

The pup immediately turned in a circle, flopped down with his nose tucked under his paws and began to snore.

Rose peered around the trunk of the biggest

tree as if she was looking for something. 'Where are the beds?'

Flax didn't answer. She was climbing into the lower branches, looking for a nice spot to curl up.

We'll get a couple of hours' sleep and set off again just after dawn, she thought.

And she closed her eyes.

Have you ever noticed that important things often happen just *before* dawn?

That silver-grey hour is one of the edges of the day.

It is when armies attack. When witches are at their most powerful. When wild creatures with sharp teeth are on the hunt.

Remember the edges.

Remember that some are more perilous than others.

CHAPTER 22
Lost

Flax couldn't sleep. She was curled up in a tree, which was where minch-wiggins had bedded down since the beginning of time. But it wasn't the right *sort* of tree.

It smelt wrong.

It felt wrong.

It even sounded wrong. The wrong sort of birds were singing up the dawn. The wrong sort of frogs croaked in the distance.

Flax sighed and looked up at the gradually lightening sky. It was too big, and too far away, and it made her feel small and lost—

No, not that sort of lost. Minch-wiggins always know exactly where they are.

But there are other sorts of lost.

When you are far from home, for example, and everything around you is strange.

Or when you have been imprisoned for many years and see no chance of escape...

What? No, of course Flax was not imprisoned. I never said she was. I was just – thinking aloud.

'We're going home,' Flax reminded herself. 'Today I'll turn us due south, and hope the pup's too busy talking to notice. And I'll lose Rose along the way somehow.'

It wasn't kind, to lose someone on purpose. But it wasn't kind to make a minch-wiggin go chasing after a dragon, either. Or to leave the Floating Forest without its only surviving Spellhound.

Flax turned over and tried to get comfortable.

She wriggled her toes.

She yawned.

Her eyes closed.

Oh good, she thought. *I'm going to sleep at last—*

Her eyes sprang open again.

The world had fallen silent. The birds in the hedge had stopped twittering. The distant frogs had stopped croaking.

Flax grabbed her satchel and sword, and slid down the tree trunk.

'Pup!' she hissed.

The pup snored on.

She was just about to pinch his ear when a quiet voice said, 'Flax? Can you smell – um – scorching?'

She spun around. Rose was staring up at the sky.

A dreadful chill touched Flax's heart. *She* looked up, too – and up and up and up.

She began to tremble.

High above their heads, something was flying north.

Something huge, with spiky wings.

Rose gasped. 'It's – it's a *dragon*!'

CHAPTER 23
The Dragon

Queens were not supposed to gape. But Rose did it all the same. She stood there with her mouth open, gazing up at the most beautiful creature she had ever seen.

The new books in the palace library made dragons sound awkward and clumsy. They said things like, 'It is an unnatural creature, like a toad with wings.'

And, 'No one knows how such an ungainly beast can fly.'

And, 'There has never been such an ugly animal, in both form and character.'

But this dragon...

This dragon was a wonder to behold. Its wings swept across the sky with lazy grace. Its head was sinuous and clever. Its scales were red-gold in the pre-dawn light.

'Oh,' whispered Rose. 'Oh oh *oh*.'

And even though this might be the very same dragon that had stolen her parents, she could not help admiring it.

Beside her, Flax was fumbling her satchel onto her back and whispering, 'I'm going home. I don't care what anyone else does. Maybe Grandpa was wrong; maybe there's no such thing as *griv*. But if there is, it can't be nearly as bad as a dragon.'

Rose didn't want her to go. Not because Flax was a nice, friendly pixie—

No, not a pixie. A minch-wiggin, whatever that was. And definitely not a friendly one. Right from the start, Flax had made it clear that she didn't want Rose tagging along.

But if Flax went, the pup would go, too. And Rose would be left alone.

Though probably not for long. Right at this moment, one of the maids would be creeping into the royal bedchamber to lay out the Queen's clothes for the day.

There would be screaming when they found her gone.

There would be panic, and a desperate hunt.

And when they found her, they'd take her back to the palace, where Aunt Delilah would be furious with her for causing so much trouble. And everyone would call her Felicia and her days would be filled with signing letters and meeting ambassadors.

But for once, Rose didn't care.

Because she had seen a dragon.

Without taking her eyes off the sky, she dipped her fingers into her pocket, found her emergency supply of green jellybabies and popped two of them in her mouth.

She had barely started chewing when she saw something puzzling.

'Is that a rope?' she whispered. 'Flax, I think the dragon is towing something.'

Even as she spoke, the sky darkened, as if the deepest part of the night had suddenly returned.

'It looks like a storm cloud,' whispered Rose. 'Though I've never seen one so big. Why would a dragon be towing a storm cloud?'

Flax gasped – and let out a groan of horror. 'It's not a storm cloud. It's the Floating Forest. The dragon has stolen my home!'

CHAPTER 24
How Frightened They Must Be

Flax stood on the same spot for a long, long time, staring after the Floating Forest. It was almost lost in the distance now, like the merest wisp of cloud.

She thought of her brother Bean, her cousin Violet, and her aunties and uncles.

How frightened they must be.

She thought of the sketters, the mor-kits, the horned globs, the owls, the frogs...

This is griv, she thought. *I didn't get the pup back to the forest quickly enough.*

And she groaned again, because she had failed so badly.

The sound woke the pup at last. He stood up in a sprawl of legs, yawned, and bounced up to Flax and Rose. 'Do you think we'll get there today? Do you think so? Huh?'

'Pup,' said Flax, 'the dragon has stolen the Floating Forest. We saw it being towed across the sky.'

She thought he'd let out one of those anguished howls, and be just as unhappy as she was. She *wanted* him to be as unhappy as she was.

Instead, he thought for a moment, flopped one ear forward and said, 'It makes no difference.'

'What do you mean it makes no difference?' cried Flax. 'Of course it makes a difference. We can't go home—'

Rose interrupted her. 'Excuse me, what's the Floating Forest? It didn't look at all like a forest to me. Are you sure it wasn't a storm cloud?'

You are probably thinking that the Queen needs

spectacles. After all, the smallest child can tell the difference between a forest and a storm cloud, even when it is so high in the sky that they almost have to fall over backwards to see it. So a ten-year-old with good eyesight should have no trouble at all.

But those who live in the Floating Forest know that it looks like a storm cloud to anyone who *doesn't* live there.

That is one of its secrets. That is how it keeps itself safe.

Or rather, how it *kept* itself safe. Because it certainly wasn't safe now.

'We can't go home,' said Flax, ignoring Rose. 'Because home isn't there anymore!'

'But we weren't going home,' said the pup. 'We were going to find the dragon. And when we find the dragon, we'll find the Floating Forest, as well as my parents.'

Flax couldn't believe he was taking it so calmly. 'But what will we *do* when we find the dragon?'

'You'll fight it,' said the pup, as if it was the most obvious thing in the world. 'With your famous sword and your amazing magic.'

'Magic?' said Rose. 'What magic?'

'Let me think,' mumbled Flax. 'I have to think.' And she hurried away to the other side of a hedge, where she could be by herself with no one saying ridiculous things like, 'You'll fight the dragon.'

But once she got there, the pup's words wouldn't leave her alone. They rang in her ears. They made her tremble all over. They reminded her that home wasn't there anymore.

She tried to imagine living in the World Below. Not just passing through for a little while; actually *living* there. Forever. With hardly any trees, and too much sky, and no magic in the land at all. With no cousins and brothers and aunties and uncles. With all those humans, most of whom were even bigger than Rose.

It was such a dreadful thought that for the first time, Flax began to wonder exactly *how* a not-very-brave minch-wiggin might fight a dragon.

How she might fight – and win.

She looked at her famous sword. She looked at her bulging satchel.

She swallowed.

'Maybe – maybe if we could find a thunderstorm?' she whispered. 'And the pup could do that thing Spellhounds do?'

Maybe then they'd have a chance. A very small one.

Flax swallowed again. 'I – I'm going to fight the dragon,' she whispered.

CHAPTER 25
The Sword

With a shaking hand, Flax drew the sword from its sheath. 'I'm going to fight,' she whispered.

And she slashed at the bottom of the hedge.

The sword sliced through twigs and leaves. 'Take that,' said Flax.

She slashed again. 'And that!'

But when she tried a third time, the sword seemed heavier than before.

A *lot* heavier.

Flax gritted her teeth and used both hands instead of one.

Slash through the twigs.

And *slash*.

And *slash!*

'I can do it,' muttered Flax. 'I can fight. I just have to keep practising.'

The sword twitched in her hand. Then it cleared its throat and said—

Thank you, I am aware that swords do not have a throat.

Or rather, *most* swords do not have a throat.

But this sword is about to speak, yes? So it must have a throat. And a larynx. And a tongue and a mouth.

Where are they? I have no idea. Perhaps they are invisible.

Anyway, this is a story. In stories, swords are allowed to clear their throats.

The sword cleared its throat and said plaintively, 'Why must it always be about fighting? Why can't I be a table sword?'

Flax was so astonished that she dropped it and skipped several steps backwards.

Then she crept forward again, peered down at the fallen blade and whispered, 'You can *talk*?'

'Of course I can talk,' said the sword. 'You heard me, didn't you? Why do minch-wiggins ask such silly questions?'

'Grandpa never said you could talk.'

'Grandpa?' said the sword. 'Was he the one before you? Restful chap? Never mentioned fighting? Never wielded me in anger?'

'That sounds like him,' said Flax.

'Well then,' said the sword, 'there was no need for me to talk to him. In fact, I may have dozed off for a few years. But now I am awake, and I ask you again, why can't I be a table sword? I'm sure it would be delightful. I could cut up cakes and slice sandwiches.'

'I don't need a table sword,' said Flax. 'How am I supposed to fight a dragon with a table sword?'

'Fight a *dragon*? Oh no. Absolutely not. Out of the question. You need a dragon-fighting sword.'

'That's you!'

'No it's not. I'm a carry-on-your-back-to-impress-the-neighbours sword. Never seen a dragon in my life.'

The more the sword talked, the more frightened and confused Flax became. 'You *are* a dragon-fighting sword! You were passed down from my great-great-great-great-great-great-great-great-great-great-great-great-great-great-great-great-great-grandmother for just that reason. She used you to fight a dragon.'

'Are you sure you've got the right number of greats?' murmured the sword. 'Perhaps you missed one. It's dreadfully easy to—'

'I don't *care* if I missed one,' shouted Flax. 'The dragon has stolen the Floating Forest, and we have to get it back!'

'Not a chance,' said the sword.

And when Flax tried to pick it up, it was so heavy that she couldn't even lift it off the ground.

CHAPTER 26
What's a Spellhound?

The thrill of seeing the dragon was beginning to wear off, and Rose was feeling hungry, tired and sore.

She had never slept on the ground before. She had never even *thought* of sleeping on the ground. And if she had thought of it, she would have assumed it would be soft and comfortable.

Because she was the Queen, and everything she had ever slept on had been soft and comfortable.

But the ground beneath the tree was littered with stones. And no matter how many Rose had dug out from under her shoulder and her hip and her head, there had always been more.

And even if there *hadn't* been stones, the ground itself was unforgiving and cold. There were no pillows. There were no feather quilts.

Rose thought of her enormous bed, which had *six* pillows and as many quilts as she wanted. And for a moment she was glad she'd be found soon, and taken back to the palace...

But then she remembered the dragon.

All over again, the wonder of it sizzled through her blood. And the same sense of wildness that had driven her to climb out the window made her forget about pillows and quilts.

But she couldn't forget how hungry she was.

'Where's Flax?' she asked. 'Why hasn't she come back yet?'

'Don't know,' answered the pup, who was busy scratching himself with one enormous hind paw.

'Well then, when is breakfast?'

'When we find it.'

'How do you *find* breakfast? Doesn't it just –

arrive? On a silver tray with silver cutlery, and a napkin tucked into a silver ring?'

The pup stopped scratching and pricked his ears. 'Flax is good at finding breakfast. But not as good as my parents. If they were here, they'd go hunting and come back with a horned glob.' He licked his lips. 'Are you hungry? I'm hungry.'

'What's a horned glob?' asked Rose.

No doubt you are asking yourself the same question.

Not because horned globs are one of the Three Great Secrets, like the Spellhounds. But because they are found only in the Floating Forest.

It is true that, every now and again, one of them wanders too close to the edge and falls down into the World Below.

But no horned glob has ever survived the fall. And if you stumbled upon the carcass, you would probably think it was a dead cow with very short legs.

Or a wild boar that had been caught in a tornado and turned inside out.

Or some sort of fungus. With horns.

And then you would go away and forget about it. Because that's how horned globs protect themselves.

They are not fierce or clever. They can't run fast. Their horns are useless in any sort of fight.

But they are very, very forgettable.

Except to Spellhounds, who never forget anything.

'What's a horned glob?' asked Rose.

'My favourite breakfast,' said the pup. He looked at her hopefully. 'Have *you* got anything to eat? Huh? Huh?'

'Only green jellybabies,' said Rose.

She took a paper bag containing her emergency supply from her pocket. She held it out to him – then pulled it back again. 'I'll give you a jellybaby if you tell me what sort of dog you are.'

'I'm not supposed to say,' said the pup, cocking his head to one side.

Rose waved the bag of jellybabies under his nose.

The pup licked his lips. He looked around for Flax. 'I'm a Spellhound.'

Rose felt another fizz of excitement. That was the word in Aunt Delilah's letter!

'What's a Spellhound?' she asked, hoping this time she'd get an answer.

'Me,' said the pup. 'And my mother and father.' He nosed at her hand. 'Can I have a jellybaby now?'

'In a minute,' said Rose. 'Um – what *makes* you a Spellhound? Apart from being able to talk?'

The pup's brow creased. 'I think it's a secret.'

Rose took a jellybaby from the bag and popped it into her mouth. 'Mm, yummy.'

The pup licked his lips again. He flattened his ears. He said quick and low, 'We *mumble mumble mumble*. We *mumble* thunder and *mumble mumble* lightning.'

And although she asked him a dozen times, he wouldn't repeat it.

So in the end she sighed and held out the jellybabies.

The pup's tongue looped out. He swallowed and wagged his tail. 'That was nice. Have you got any more?'

Rose stared at her empty hand. 'You ate all of them. Including the paper bag.'

'What's a paper bag?' asked the pup.

CHAPTER 27
I Hope Someone Nice Picks Me Up

Flax sat beside the sword with her head in her hands.

Right from the start, she had known she wasn't a proper Destroyer-of-Dragons-and-Protector-of-her-People.

She wasn't particularly brave.

She wasn't particularly clever.

That wouldn't have mattered if the dragon hadn't come. Like Grandpa, she could have worn the sword all her life, without ever having to wield it.

But the dragon *had* come. And it had stolen her home, along with all her cousins and aunties and uncles.

She looked at the sword for the last time, wishing she was the sort of person who could persuade it to help her.

Then she stood up and walked away.

Behind her, the sword murmured, 'I hope someone nice picks me up. A baker, perhaps. Someone who will use me to cut cake.'

Flax stopped. She wasn't brave, but maybe she could be just a little bit clever.

'You don't look like a cake-cutting sword,' she said over her shoulder. 'I expect someone strong and fierce will find you. Like a human soldier.'

She heard a faint clang, as if the sword had accidentally knocked against a rock.

'What do you mean, a soldier?' it called after her. 'Soldiers use cannons and guns. A soldier wouldn't want a silly old sword. Besides, humans are enormous. They'd probably use me for a butter knife. I wouldn't mind being a butter knife.'

'I've heard that human soldiers carry all sorts of weapons,' said Flax, who knew nothing at all about human soldiers or what they carried. 'Because they never know what's going to happen in the heat of battle.'

'Battle?' The sword's voice rose to a squeak. 'You mean, blood and slaughter? Lots of screaming? Everyone running around chopping off legs and arms? No, I won't agree to it.'

'You mightn't get a choice,' said Flax. 'Humans are awfully big and strong. They could probably carry you into battle whether you wanted it or not.'

She heard another clang, louder this time.

When she turned around, the sword had disappeared.

In its place was a spoon.

'There,' said the spoon. 'No one will even think of carrying me into battle now.'

Flax goggled at it. 'You can change shape? As well as talk?'

'I have many talents,' the spoon said smugly.

'Then yes,' said Flax, 'a soldier will love you.

They can carry you into battle during the day, and use you to eat their supper at night.'

And she turned away again.

'Wait!' cried the spoon. 'I – I might have been a little hasty. When you said fight a dragon, perhaps you meant an itsy-bitsy one? Like a – a dragonette?'

Flax shook her head. 'I wish it *was* itsy-bitsy. But it's really big. And powerful enough to tow the Floating Forest through the sky.'

The spoon mumbled to itself for a moment or two. Then, 'All right, but when you said *fight*, did you mean walk straight up to it? Like, "Ho, enormous fire-spitting dragon, I challenge you to mortal combat"?'

'No!' said Flax, horrified. 'I meant sneak around behind it and hope it doesn't see me. I don't *want* to fight. I *won't* fight, not if I can help it. I just want to be prepared.'

With a sigh, the spoon became a sword again. 'In that case,' it said in a subdued tone, 'I think we can come to an arrangement.'

Fighting with a sword is actually very simple. You just grasp it by one end, and hit your opponent with the other.

It is more complicated, of course, if your opponent does not want to be hit.

Or if he is a dragon.

CHAPTER 28
Secrets

They set off again, heading north.

Really heading north this time, instead of pretending-to-go-north-while-gradually-twisting-around-to-the-south.

With every step she took, Flax felt weighed down with secrets.

First, and worst, was the Dark and Terrible Secret.

It had been bad enough before. But now they were actually going *towards* the dragon, instead of sneaking away from it, it seemed Darker. And even more Terrible.

She tried not to think about it, but that just

left room for the other secrets to come crowding in around her.

The fact that the pup was a Spellhound. Which Rose must not discover, because she was human and Flax didn't trust her.

The fact that the sword could talk. *And* change shape. Which Rose must not discover (because she was human and Flax didn't trust her). And which the pup wasn't going to hear about because he might tell Rose.

The fact that Flax was scared out of her wits.

'How did this happen?' she whispered to herself. 'I'm just an ordinary minch-wiggin. I'm not meant to carry this many secrets.'

She wondered if she should try again to get rid of Rose. Except she couldn't think how. And besides, maybe the pup was right when he said three was better than two.

It wasn't a *lot* better. Not against a dragon. Three hundred might make a difference. Or three thousand.

But just three?

Flax shivered, and tried not to think about that, too.

A little way ahead of her, the pup was poking his nose into everything he passed. Flowers. Brambles. Holes in the ground.

'Can we eat this, Flax?' he asked. 'How about this? How about this?'

Flax glanced towards him, just as Rose cried, 'No, it's a wasp, keep away from it!'

'Ow!' The pup pawed at his nose and whimpered, 'It bit me! Ow-ow-ow!'

Some of the plants in the World Below were strange; others were almost familiar. Flax grabbed something that looked like wild garlic and crushed it with her bare heel.

'Stand still,' she said to the pup.

'But it hurts! OW-OW-OW-OW-OW!'

In a distant field, a couple of humans looked up from their work, as if they had heard something.

Flax grabbed one of the pup's ears and pulled

his head down. She squeezed the crushed garlic onto his nose.

Gradually, he stopped crying.

Rose watched open-mouthed. 'How did you know what to do?'

'Everyone knows garlic is good for wasp stings,' said Flax. She glared at the pup. 'And everyone knows you shouldn't try to eat wasps! Look, there's the nest in that tree. You're lucky the whole lot of them didn't come after you.'

'I was hungry,' mumbled the pup.

'Then help me find some acorns,' said Flax. 'And thistles.'

Rose made a squeaking sound. 'You eat *thistles* for breakfast? Couldn't we find some porridge with brown sugar and cream? Or eggs and toast? And maybe a little bit of cake?'

'Does porridge grow on trees, like acorns?' asked the pup. 'Is it nice? Is it as nice as horned glob?' He pawed his nose one last time, as if to make sure it didn't hurt any more. Then he stood up and wagged his tail. 'What about cake? Can we find a cake tree?'

'No, someone has to cook it,' said Rose.

'How?'

'I – I'm not sure. Qu – quite ordinary fourth chambermaids don't do much cooking.'

But then she brightened. 'Maybe you could catch a rabbit.'

'What's a rabbit?' asked the pup.

Rose shaded her eyes against the early morning sun and studied the nearby fields. 'There!' she cried. 'That's a rabbit!'

The pup let out a yelp of excitement and bolted after a small furry creature with long ears.

The humans in the distant field turned and watched him.

The pup was very fast. For a moment, Flax thought he was going to catch the rabbit.

But then it dodged, and the pup couldn't stop in time. He ploughed straight into a bush and ended up in a tangle of leaves, branches and legs.

The rabbit disappeared down a hole.

Flax and Rose pulled the pup out of the bush and brushed away the twigs and leaves. The pup shook himself. 'I nearly caught it,' he said. 'I'll get the next one.'

'You'll have to be quieter with the next one,' said Flax. 'I think the *can't-see-us-can't-hear-us-can't-smell-us* is wearing off.'

The pup stared at her. 'Can't you do your magic again?'

'You *did* say magic before!' Rose's eyes were wide. 'How does it work? Can you make us invisible?'

Flax hunched her shoulders. 'No. I have to keep it to fight the dragon.'

'But you've got so much,' said the pup, peering at her bulging satchel. 'Can't you spare a bit?'

'I told you, no,' snapped Flax. 'Just – try to look smaller, can't you?'

The pup did his best to look smaller. But then he started sniffing things again. He sniffed this way and that. He cocked his head and stared at a tree. He took a long time jumping over a fence.

At last, he pinned back his ears and said, 'We came past here last night, Flax. We're going in the wrong direction. We're supposed to be going north after the dragon.'

'We *are* going north after the dragon,' said Flax, without looking at him.

The pup stopped. 'But that means – that means last night we were going *away* from the dragon.'

Rose stopped too. 'We were?'

The pup whined softly. 'Why were we going away from the dragon last night, Flax? Don't you want to find my parents?'

'Maybe I got turned around,' mumbled Flax. 'Maybe I got the direction wrong.'

'Minch-wiggins *never* get the direction wrong,' said the pup.

'Never ever?' asked Rose.

'Never ever,' said the pup.

He didn't say another word for the rest of

the day. He ate acorns and thistles and seeds without complaint.

But every time he looked at Flax, his eyes were big with hurt and betrayal.

CHAPTER 29
Soooo Hungry

The pup was hungry. Soooooo hungry.

Acorns and thistles and mushrooms might be fine for Flax. (*Treacherous* Flax.) And Rose seemed to be getting used to them (though she still wished aloud for cake, or porridge-and-cream, or roast-venison-with-gravy).

But they weren't nearly enough for a growing Spellhound pup.

What he *really* wanted was to catch a rabbit. He thought about it every morning before they set off, and every night before he went to sleep, just after he thought about his parents.

What's that?

Yes, several days have passed.

Why didn't I say so?

I just did.

How many days exactly?

I have no idea. I heard this part of the story from the pup, and Spellhounds are notoriously bad at keeping track of time. All the pup could tell me was that they had gone up and down a lot of hills, crossed a lot of streams and avoided a lot of humans.

What, you *still* want to know how many days?

Very well, let us say five.

No, I have no idea if that's right! I told you—

Look, just sit down and be quiet. We are coming to a *very important* part of the story.

In the past *five days*, the pup had chased many rabbits, with ears pricked and mouth watering.

But he hadn't caught a single one. They dodged. They dived. They doubled back in the most unexpected fashion.

Then they disappeared down their burrows.

The pup wished he had time to stop and dig them out. But he *couldn't* stop, not while the dragon had his parents. So, each time, he snuffled and snorted at the mouth of the burrow, then hurried after Rose and Flax. (*Treacherous* Flax.)

On this particular morning, as they walked up a steep hill and down the other side, he had a brilliant idea.

'When I get my parents back,' he said to Rose, 'they can teach me how to catch rabbits. I can practise all the way home. And by the time we get to the Floating Forest, I'll be able to do it.'

'The dragon has the Floating Forest,' said Flax. 'Home will be right there.'

The pup didn't want to admit she was right,

so he sat down and scratched, which always helped him think. He scratched behind his right ear. He scratched behind his left ear—

Then he scrambled to his feet, thinking, *I'll ask my parents if we can stay in the World Below for a little while. Just long enough for me to learn to catch a rabbit!*

It was such an exciting thought that when he caught up with Flax and Rose again, he bounced around them three times.

Or rather, he bounced around Rose. He definitely didn't bounce around Flax.

'Hey, Rose,' he panted. 'Are we nearly there? How far to go? Are we close? Huh? Huh?'

Rose looked at the hill behind them. She looked at the river that lay at the bottom of the hill, and the odd-shaped mountain that loomed a little way ahead, its peak hidden in cloud.

'I think that must be Mount Tangle,' she said. 'So yes, we're nearly there.'

'That's where the dragon lives?' asked Flax. 'Mount Tangle?'

Rose nodded. 'It said so in the book. It said dragons have lived at Mount Tangle forever.'

Flax folded her ears back. 'How old was this book?'

'I only read the first page.'

'So you don't know how old it was?' asked Flax.

'Well—' said Rose.

'Yes?' The pup wagged his tail.

'It was – old-ish.'

'*How* old-ish?' demanded Flax. 'Ten years? Twenty?'

'A bit more than twenty.' Rose's face was red, and she was biting her lip.

'How much more?' asked Flax.

'Um – about – five hundred years?'

Flax let out a squeak of dismay. Then she and Rose began to argue about whether the dragon would still be living in the same place after five hundred years.

The pup didn't like arguments. So he set off to look for rabbits.

Flax called after him. 'Don't go too far. And don't go near any humans; remember they can see you.'

The pup stuck his nose in the air. He wasn't going to listen to Flax. (*Treacherous* Flax.) He would go as far as he liked.

But before he found a single rabbit, he smelled something on the wind; something so glorious that he started drooling on the spot.

Right there and then he decided it was his new favourite smell. His nose headed straight towards it, and the pup followed.

He didn't think of danger – how could a smell like that be dangerous? He didn't think of anything except *food*.

The source of the smell turned out to be a pile of meat strips, set on the ground beneath a tree. The pup galloped towards it. His stomach made excited noises. His tongue tried to get there faster than the rest of him.

The meat tasted as good as it smelled. He was

gulping it down as quickly as he could when a voice above him hissed, 'Now!'

And a web of knotted rope dropped around him.

CHAPTER 30
A Desperate Howl

Flax was still arguing with Rose when she heard the pup yelp with fright.

At first she thought he must've run headfirst into a bush again, and she kept arguing.

But then he howled. There were no words, just a long, desperate, 'OooooOOOOOOOOOOOoooh!'

Flax ran towards the sound.

So did Rose.

The human girl's legs were much longer than the minch-wiggin's, and as she passed Flax, she bent down and picked her up.

Then she kept running.

On any other occasion, Flax would have

protested. (It is *very* bad manners to pick up a minch-wiggin without first asking permission.)

But the pup was in trouble. So Flax wrapped her tail around Rose's wrist and held on tight.

As they approached a thicket of trees at the bottom of the hill, she heard another yelp.

'He's just past the trees,' she hissed. 'Don't rush in. We don't know what's happening.'

Rose slowed to a walk, and Flax scrambled up onto her shoulder. 'Through there,' she whispered, pointing.

Rose crept forward, hidden by the trees.

And there was the pup, covered in ropes. There was one around his nose and another around his neck. There were three around his legs, pulled tight to stop him kicking. And four or five more, wrapped around him every which way to make sure he could not escape.

Two very large human men were dragging him towards a black automobile.

Rose gasped.

'Put me down,' whispered Flax.

'You can't fight them,' whispered Rose. 'They're too big.'

Flax had no intention of fighting anyone. 'Put me down!'

Rose lowered her to the ground, and Flax crept out from among the trees.

At this point it is worth mentioning that everyone and everything who lives in the Floating Forest has a small amount of magic in them.

Most of it is in the trees. But other creatures have it, too. They breathe it in with the air. They drink it with the water.

Mor-kits use it to grow their hunting teeth.

Horned globs use it to make themselves more forgettable.

Minch-wiggins use it to creep unseen through shadows.

But to creep unseen through shadows, there must first *be* shadows.

Flax did her best. She found shadows so small that she had to crouch almost double to stay hidden. She found shadows so thin that she had to suck in her breath so as not to be seen.

But the day was too bright. And the automobile was too far away from the trees. Ahead of her, the pup was struggling against his ropes.

'Don't let it escape,' cried one of the men. 'We want the reward.'

The other man cursed, and pulled the ropes tighter.

Then the two of them wrapped their arms around the pup and, with much grunting and groaning, lifted him into the back of the automobile.

The first man slammed the door, dusted himself down and chuckled. 'We've earned our money here, Derk.'

'There's not a dog in this world that can resist the smell of bacon,' said Derk.

'It's a fine, powerful beast,' said the first man. 'I'm tempted to keep it.'

Derk shook his head. 'You don't want to get on the wrong side of the Lady. Come on, let's get out of here.'

Flax tried to go faster. But now there wasn't a single shadow to be found, and she was right out in the open. If the men turned their heads...

Derk and the other man climbed into the front of the automobile.

Flax forgot about shadows and raced towards it.

The automobile made a growling sound and sprang forward. So did Flax, trying to grab hold of something—

But her fingers slid off the shiny blackness, and she fell in a heap.

She fell.

And the automobile roared away, taking the Spellhound pup with it.

CHAPTER 31
The Wisdom of Hindsight

Let me tell you what Flax *should* have done.

As soon as she saw the pup, trussed up and helpless, she should have reached into her satchel, taken out a thread of magic, and tied a knot too small to see.

Then she would not have had to worry about shadows. She could have run full tilt towards the two men, and they would not have known she was there.

She could have reached the pup in time to draw her sword and cut him free.

Meanwhile Rose (who is really Queen Felicia), could have thrown sticks and twigs and branches to distract the men...

Ah, but this is the wisdom of hindsight.

It is so easy, afterwards, to think of all the things we could have done.

The things we *should* have done.

But it is much harder in the heat of the moment. Especially if you are a minch-wiggin, and not used to quick thinking.

Or a queen, who has never been in such a dangerous situation before.

(Actually, she has. But she was much too young to remember it.)

'I should've used magic,' groaned Flax. 'If I'd made myself invisible, I wouldn't have had to worry about shadows. Then I could have saved him.' She put her head in her hands. 'But I didn't think of it.'

'I should have thrown something at them,' cried Rose. 'I should have lured them away from the automobile to give you time. But *I* didn't think of it either.'

'And now he's gone,' whispered Flax.

They sat in despairing silence. Flax was thinking about how scared the pup must be. She was wondering who the Lady was, and why someone would offer a reward for the pup when humans weren't even supposed to know about him. And why oh *why* hadn't she thought of using her magic to get to him in ti—

'Oh!' she squeaked. She sat bolt upright and unbuckled her satchel with trembling fingers.

'What are you doing?' asked Rose.

'We're going after them,' said Flax.

She forgot about not trusting Rose. She forgot that other humans mustn't see her. It was too late for such caution.

She took a *very* small thread from the satchel. She grasped the ends of it and tied a knot.

She tied it so quickly that she almost dropped it; so fast that her fingers became a blur.

Then she scrambled up onto Rose's shoulder, took a firm hold on the collar of her coat, and swallowed the thread.

'Run,' she said. 'Run after the automobile.'

Rose stared at her. 'But I can't—'

'Just *run*!' cried Flax.

Rose stood up uncertainly. She took a step forward.

She took another step. And another.

She began to run.

CHAPTER 32
Magic

Rose was running so fast it felt like flying.

She had never had anything to do with magic before—

Actually, she had. But she was much too young to remember it.

She had never had anything to do with magic before, and it thrilled her.

Her feet skimmed over the road. The wind whistled past her ears. Her heart sang.

When they came to a large village she pulled up her collar and kept her head down so no one would recognise her from the coins and stamps, and kept running.

She flew past an inn, a school, and a row of shops. Women turned and stared. A man shouted in astonishment. A trio of boys tried in vain to catch her.

Rose raced past them all with Flax clinging to her collar and the tiny sword banging against her shoulder.

'Faster,' cried the minch-wiggin, and her voice was whisked away by the wind. 'Faster!'

They caught up with a red automobile and passed it, while the passengers goggled at them. They passed a green automobile that nearly ran off the road when the driver saw them.

They passed a black automobile, but it was the wrong one.

And then they came to a crossroads.

Rose stopped so abruptly that Flax nearly lost her grip.

'Which way?' asked Rose. 'Which way should we go?'

Flax mumbled something that Rose couldn't hear. She nodded. She shook her head, as if she was arguing with herself.

Then she unbuckled her satchel and took out another tiny thread.

The knot she tied was so complicated that Rose had to blink and blink again to keep track of it. But just as she thought Flax had completely lost the end of the thread, it turned up in the right place.

'Magic,' whispered Rose. Her fingers tingled with excitement.

'*Finding* magic,' said Flax, and she swallowed the thread.

She looked at the three roads ahead of them. She pointed to the one on the left, which was lined on either side with pine trees. 'There!'

Rose leapt forward again.

They passed through another village, smaller and dustier than the last one. And another, which was almost in the foothills of Mount Tangle—

'Stop!' squeaked Flax, right in Rose's ear.

Just past the village, there was a narrow side road with a few houses scattered along it.

'Down there,' whispered Flax. 'But go carefully. We're close.'

Rose crept down the road, hoping they wouldn't run into anyone. They passed the first house, which had a tumbledown shed beside it.

'Not that one,' whispered Flax.

They passed the second house, which was painted bright yellow.

'Not that one, either.'

The third house had a pine hedge in front of it, and a driveway leading into a wooden garage.

'This is the one,' whispered Flax. She pointed to the garage. 'The pup's in there.'

Rose sidled past the hedge, her heart beating furiously. She half expected Aunt Delilah to step out from behind the house and snap, 'A queen does *not* behave like a burglar!'

But there was no sign of Aunt Delilah.

And Rose *was* behaving like a burglar.

She ducked past a window, holding her breath. She peeped around the back corner of the house. She tiptoed towards the garage.

The side of it that faced away from the house

was blackened at the bottom, as if there had been a small fire. The garage door was shut – and locked with a shiny new padlock.

'What do we do now?' whispered Rose.

Flax unsheathed her sword, and was talking to it. 'A key,' she whispered. 'Can you be a key?'

To Rose's astonishment, the sword began to change shape. It bulged on one side, and then on the other, in a slightly different place.

It began to look very much like a key.

'How did you do that?' whispered Rose.

Flax didn't answer. She climbed down Rose's arm and slid the key into the padlock.

But then she froze. At the back of the house, a door creaked open.

'That was her on the phone,' Derk said loudly. 'She wants us to bring the dog to her. I'll get the automobile out.'

CHAPTER 33
What are We Going to *Do*?

Flax whipped the key out of the padlock, and Rose hurried around the corner of the garage just in time.

Heavy footsteps tramped towards them and stopped at the garage door.

'What are we going to *do*?' breathed Rose.

'I don't know!'

Flax wanted to run in circles. She wanted to hide under the nearest bush until everything sorted itself out.

But it *wouldn't* sort itself out, not without a bit of help.

Derk unlocked the garage doors and dragged

them open. Flax heard him climb into the automobile.

It rumbled out of the garage and stopped in the
driveway.

'Think of something,' hissed Rose.

But Flax couldn't think of a single useful thing.

Derk shouted above the rumble of the
automobile, 'Hurry up, Gav. Don't want to keep
her waiting.'

'Yeah yeah,' came the reply from somewhere
inside the house. 'I'll be with you in a minute.'

Rose was jiggling from foot to foot. 'What can
we do? What can we—'

She stopped and peered down at the blackened
boards, where there had once been a small fire.
'The dragon,' she whispered.

She dumped Flax on the ground, picked up a
piece of burnt wood and rubbed it all over her face.

She rubbed it on her coat, too, until she looked
as if *she* had been in a fire. She tore off a couple of
buttons.

'Gav!' shouted Derk. 'Hurry up!'

'Coming,' shouted Gav.

The back door of the house slammed, and a different set of footsteps hurried towards the automobile.

Rose took a shaky breath, rumpled her hair – and screamed, 'Heeeelp! The dragon! The dragon's after me!'

She stumbled around the corner of the garage, waving her arms. 'Heeeeelp! Save me! It's the dragon!'

Derk cursed. 'The automobile won't protect us,' he shouted. 'Not against a dragon. Back to the house, Gav. Go!'

'What about the girl?'

'Who cares about the girl? With any luck the dragon'll eat her and forget about us.'

The two men threw themselves out of the automobile and pounded back the way they had come. The door of the house opened and slammed shut again.

Flax raced out of hiding. Rose picked her up and ran to the automobile, screeching, 'It's going to kill me. Help meeeee!'

The pup was still tied up in the back seat. When Rose threw open the door, he moaned with fright.

Flax leapt down beside him. 'Rope cutting,' she whispered to the key.

It twitched in her hand and was a sword again, its blade sharp and gleaming.

'Hurry!' hissed Rose.

Flax slashed at the ropes, while Rose banged on the roof of the automobile and screeched, 'Aaaaaaargh! It's here! AAAAAAAARGH!'

The pup's legs were so cramped from being tied up that he fell out of the car and onto the ground.

He whimpered, 'The dragon. It's going to get us.'

'It's a trick,' whispered Flax. 'But they'll figure it out soon. Hurry, pup. Please hurry. Can you walk yet?'

'I think so,' said the pup. And with a bit of help

from Rose, he climbed to his feet and staggered up the driveway, with Flax trotting alongside.

'Hurry,' she said. 'We've got to hurry!'

By then, the cramp was beginning to wear off, and the pup could go a little faster. Rose picked Flax up again and they trotted down the road until the house with the hedge was out of sight.

Then they struck out across the fields, heading for the foothills of Mount Tangle.

CHAPTER 34
Run for the Trees

The fields were bumpy, and dotted with rabbit holes and fences. There were a few trees, and lots of small bushes, but none big enough to hide a Spellhound. Not for long.

'They'll work out it's a trick and come after us,' said Flax. 'Pup, can you run yet?'

The pup shook himself, stretched, groaned enormously – and bounced around them twice to prove that the stiffness was gone and he was himself again.

'You saved me, Flax,' he cried. 'You saved me, Rose. You were clever!'

Rose beamed. 'I've never done anything like

it before. But it worked. We *were* clever, weren't we?'

'And we need to keep being clever,' said Flax, looking back towards the road. (Was that a shout of rage she heard, somewhere behind them? Was that the roar of an automobile?)

'Rose,' she said, 'can I ride on your shoulder again?'

Rose picked her up. Ahead of them loomed Mount Tangle, its lower slopes covered in trees, its peak still lost in clouds.

'Run,' said Flax. 'If we can get to the trees, we should be safe.'

Rose started to run – but after four steps she stopped in dismay. 'The magic's not working. I'm not fast anymore.'

'Try again,' said Flax. (That *was* the roar of an automobile.) 'Quickly!'

Rose tried again, stumbling over the lumpy ground with the pup loping beside her and Flax clinging to the collar of her coat.

But although she was much faster than a

minch-wiggin, she was nowhere near as fast as she should have been.

'What's going on?' said Rose. 'What's happened to the magic?'

Flax swallowed. 'It's worn off. The thread was too small.'

She looked over her shoulder, just as a black automobile roared out of the village and stopped by the side of the road.

And there in the distance were the two men, leaning out the windows. One of them pointed, and cried out in triumph. The other leapt out of the automobile and threw open the nearest gate.

'Just run,' cried Flax. 'We have to get to the trees.'

But the trees were still a long way off when the automobile roared through the gate and began to bump and rattle across the fields towards them.

Rose ran faster. She scrambled over a fence and kept running, though she was already puffing and panting.

The pup could have outpaced them both. But he ran beside them, wide-eyed and frightened. 'What do we do now, Flax? What do we do now, Rose? Huh? Huh?'

'More magic,' puffed Rose. 'Make me fast again. Or – no, make us invisible. You can do that, can't you, Flax?'

Flax unbuckled her satchel. She didn't *want* to use more magic. She was going to need it to fight the dragon.

But the two men mustn't recapture the pup.

She reached into the satchel; her fingers searched its depths.

Her thoughts wobbled.

'Are we invisible yet?' asked Rose.

Flax couldn't speak. The words stuck in her throat and wouldn't come out.

Behind them, the automobile rumbled over the uneven ground. The lumps and bumps and rabbit holes slowed it down, and so did the gates. But it was gaining on them. The men shouted encouragement to each other. Their voices came closer and closer.

'I—' croaked Flax.

'What's the matter?' puffed Rose.

'There's—' whispered Flax.

'There's what?' asked the pup.

'There's – there's no magic left. I've used it all.'

'But your satchel,' cried Rose. 'It's bulging.'

Flax shook her head. 'It's full of moss. There was hardly any magic there in the first place. And now there's none left to save us.'

This is the trouble with Dark and Terrible Secrets. They always reveal themselves at the worst possible moment.

And this *is* the worst possible moment. The only thing that could make the situation more dire was if there was a dragon somewhere ahead of them.

Oh, wait…

CHAPTER 35
A Plan

The pup was so shocked that he loped right past a crouching rabbit and didn't even think of trying to catch it.

'No magic?' he yelped. 'What are we going to do?'

'I don't know,' said Flax. 'But you should run, pup. It's you they want. Run as fast as you can.'

The pup's heart skipped a beat. He didn't want to leave his friends.

But Flax was clever. If she said run, he'd better run.

He veered off to one side, bounding over bushes and rabbit holes.

Behind him, Gav bellowed, 'There it goes.

After it, Derk! Don't worry about the girl.'

The pup's ears flattened in fright.

He wished his mother was here. Or his father. He wished they would appear right in front of him, so fierce and amazing that Derk and Gav would turn around and drive straight back the way they had come.

But his mother and father couldn't help him. No one could help him. He was going to have to save himself.

I have to be clever, he thought. *As clever as Flax and Rose.*

He galloped past a couple of bushes and leapt over a fence, thinking so hard that his ears hurt. How could he lose an automobile that never got tired? How could he lose two angry men, when they were so determined to catch him?

And then he saw something. And a plan crept into his mind.

He turned it over as he ran, to make sure it was a *good* plan.

Then he sped up a little.

But he had only taken a few steps when he yelped as if he'd trodden on something sharp and hurt his paw.

He looked over his shoulder and showed the whites of his eyes. He limped. He whimpered. He limped faster, desperate to escape.

The automobile roared. Gav hung out the window with the net in his hands, and his voice hoarse with excitement. 'We've got it, Derk. Don't bother with the gate. Go through the fence.'

Directly ahead of the pup was a clump of bushes with a small tree in the middle. He limped towards the bushes, as if he thought they might hide him from his pursuers.

The automobile crashed through the fence and followed him. The pup glanced back and changed direction, *away* from the bushes.

A moment later, the automobile changed direction, too. It was gaining on him; soon it would be upon him.

In desperation, the pup swung back towards the bushes, his limp worse than ever.

The automobile swerved after him. Gav was screaming, 'We've got it! We've got it!'

The pup found one last burst of strength. Despite his limp, he sped up. So did the automobile. It snapped at his heels, so close he could feel the heat of it.

He yelped with fear. He dived towards the bushes—

And at the very last moment, he leapt to one side, his limp forgotten.

Derk spun the wheel, trying to stay on his tail. But the automobile couldn't swerve as quickly as the pup. It crashed headlong into the bushes, and into the small tree that stood in the middle of them.

The branches of the tree shook violently.

So did the wasps' nest the pup had spotted.

There was an outraged buzz – and thousands of little striped bodies poured out of the nest.

Gav bellowed again, but this time it was with horror.

He dropped the net. He flailed his arms. 'Get us out of here!' he shrieked.

The automobile grumbled and heaved and hissed, but did not move. With another shriek, Gav threw open the door and scrambled out, closely followed by Derk.

The last the pup saw of them, they were running back the way they had come, chased by a swarm of angry wasps.

Perhaps we should end our story here, with the villains defeated, and our heroes triumphant.

Perhaps we should leave the rest untold.

You don't *really* want to hear about the dragon, do you?

And betrayal.

And imprisonment?

And even more Dark and Terrible Secrets?

This is a much nicer place to stop. So let us pretend this is:

THE END

There, wasn't it a lovely story? Now you can go to bed happy.

. . .

What? You want to hear the rest of it?

Well.

Don't say I didn't warn you.

CHAPTER 36
What Happened to Your Magic?

Trees, thought Flax. *Trees!*

She lay on her back, looking up at the leaves and branches that covered the lower slopes of Mount Tangle.

They weren't as nice as the leaves and branches of the Floating Forest. But they were a hundred times better than roads, towns, automobiles and angry humans.

She wanted to lie here for days.

A wet nose touched her ear. 'Flax,' said the pup in a quiet voice, 'what happened to your magic?'

Flax closed her eyes, remembering her terrible

confession. 'I'm sorry,' she whispered. 'I should have told you earlier.'

'Is it really all gone?' asked Rose.

Flax nodded. 'I only inherited a few threads from Grandpa. And even though I tried and tried, I could only catch a few more.'

'But where did it *go*?' asked the pup.

'Someone must have used it,' said Flax. 'And stuffed the satchel with moss to make up for it. I don't think it was Grandpa. Maybe it was his grandma. Or his *great* grandma. They probably thought it didn't matter, because the dragon hadn't come near us for a hundred years.'

She opened her eyes and said miserably, 'But now it *does* matter...'

'So how do we fight the dragon?' asked the pup.

'I don't know,' whispered Flax.

No one spoke for a while. Then Rose said, 'If you haven't got any magic left, how did you turn your sword into a key?'

Flax sat up and unsheathed the sword. 'It's got its own magic.'

'Of course I have,' said the sword.

The pup flattened his ears. Rose jerked back in surprise. 'Your sword can *talk*?'

The sword snorted. 'Do you have any more silly questions?'

'But – but *how* can you talk?' asked Rose. 'I've never heard of such a thing.'

'Just as I have never heard of a quite ordinary fourth chambermaid,' said the sword. 'But here we both are. Now, what do you need me to do? Cut up a sandwich? I'm good at sandwiches. Triangles or squares? Crusts on or off?'

The pup licked his lips. 'What about bacon? Derk and Gav had bacon, but it was a nasty trick. I want bacon *without* nasty tricks.'

The mention of bacon reminded Flax of something that had been worrying her.

'Those two men were working for someone. They called her the Lady—'

'The *Lady*?' shrieked the sword. '*She* is part of this? Oh no. Oh no no no no no. Sheathe me again, minch-wiggin, and hide me under a bush somewhere. Not the Lady. No no no, never the Lady.'

Flax stared at it. 'You know who she is?'

'No idea,' the sword said quickly. 'Absolutely no idea at all.'

Only now it was a cake tin. And it was trembling.

Rose leaned towards it. 'Why are you so scared?'

'Because I value my life,' snapped the cake tin. 'It's only a very small life, but it's mine, and I would like to keep it. If you had any sense, you'd be scared, too.'

'But who *is* she?' asked Flax.

The cake tin shrank a little. 'Is there anyone nearby who might overhear us? Anyone with feathers on their elbows, and silence where their heartbeat should be?'

The day seemed to grow suddenly colder. 'The Lady is a *witch*?' squeaked Flax.

'Shhh, not so loud,' whispered the cake tin. 'She is not just *a* witch. She is *the* witch. She is the leader of them all.'

I told you we should have stopped while things were going well. But you didn't listen, did you?

Listen to me now.

There is a witch in this story.

The witch.

So you must be prepared.

I suggest you leave the rest of your green jellybabies with me, and hide under the bed covers until the story is done.

It is all right to tremble.

Everyone trembles when it comes to the Lady.

CHAPTER 37
We Haven't Got Time for Secrets

Rose had known for as long as she could remember that there were witches in Hallow.

No one had actually told her so. But she had heard the whispers.

'They say Lord Buff's grandmother was a witch. Don't trust him. Don't trust any of his family.'

And, 'One of the servants found a feather in Lady Verit's bed. Lady Verit swears it fell out of her pillow. But she would say that, wouldn't she?'

And, 'Have you heard the rumours about Lady Span? They say she goes out on moonless nights, and won't tell anyone where she's been. You have to wonder, don't you?'

Sometimes, as Rose sat on her throne, listening to the gossip ebbing and flowing around her, it sounded as if half the nobles in the country were witches.

At other times, it sounded like a big fuss about nothing.

But this was different. This was real.

'Why—' It felt dangerous to even say the words. But she had to know. 'Why would the Lady want you, pup?'

The pup's ears were flat against his head, and his tail was tucked between his legs. 'Because—'

'It's a secret,' Flax said quickly. 'A *huge* secret.'

'It seems to me,' said Rose, 'that we can't afford secrets. Not anymore. Not with a dragon somewhere ahead of us, and the Lady coming along behind. It seems to me that secrets are just going to get us into more trouble.'

(She didn't mean *her* secret, about being Queen. That was different.)

Flax and the pup looked at each other. 'Rose helped save me,' said the pup.

'I know,' said Flax. 'But she's human.'

'*Nice* human,' said the pup.

'But still human,' said Flax.

'Look,' said Rose, 'I already know he's a Spellhound. And I know about the thunder and lightning.'

This was not entirely true. Rose only knew that Spellhounds had *something to do with* thunder and lightning.

But being a queen is excellent practice for lying. Rose had been gracious to the ambassador from Quill, and never once shown how much she disliked him. She had pretended to enjoy state dinners, even when the main course was tripe in white sauce and the dessert was lumpy rice pudding (the Stonehuff prime minister's two favourite dishes).

She had pretended to be fond of Aunt Delilah.

If you ever need to tell a really big lie, I suggest you first get in some training as a queen.

'Who told you about the thunder and lightning?' demanded Flax.

The pup looked guilty. So Rose said, 'I worked it out. By myself. Now, what is it that makes a witch want a Spellhound pup?'

'Well—' Flax hunched her shoulders.

'Shall I go to sleep for another couple of decades while you make up your mind?' snapped the cake tin. 'Just tell her.'

Flax looked around, as if to make sure there wasn't anyone nearby with feathers on their elbows and no heartbeat.

'So you know Spellhounds eat thunder and swallow lightning?' she whispered.

'Of course,' said Rose, though she *hadn't* known it.

She turned to the pup. 'Have *you* eaten thunder? Have you swallowed lighting?'

'Not yet,' said the pup, staring at the ground. 'But I've seen my parents do it.'

'That's how they fill themselves with power,' said Flax. 'And once they're filled up, they can make other people's magic stronger. That's why Spellhounds are such a secret. No one wants the witches to find out about them. If a witch has a Spellhound by her side, she's almost unstoppable.'

Rose felt herself go pale. An unstoppable witch? In *Hallow*?

Now *she* looked around before she spoke. 'Do you think the Lady knows the pup is a Spellhound?'

'Of course she does,' snapped the cake tin. 'Why else would a witch try to capture such a clumsy great creature? I say we go into hiding for a few years until she forgets about him. We'll find a nice village somewhere, and go to ground. The pup can pretend to be a very large dog, and I'll get a job in a bakery.'

Rose did not think of herself as brave. Queens didn't need to be brave; they had plenty of other people to do it on their behalf.

But she couldn't go into hiding. At some point she'd have to go back to being Queen, and what if the Lady found the pup *after* that? What if Rose was stuck in the palace in High Kinnick, signing letters and balancing books on her head, while an unstoppable witch rampaged through Hallow?

She shivered. 'I don't think hiding will solve anything. Not for long.'

'If we find my parents,' said the pup, 'they'll protect me from the witch.'

For the briefest of moments, Rose imagined finding her *own* parents. Still alive after all these years, and waiting for her to rescue them from the dragon.

She imagined them smiling at her. Throwing their arms around her. Loving her as no one had loved her for as long as she could remember.

She didn't let herself think about it for long. But it lingered in the corner of her mind. And it was definitely one of the reasons why she gathered her courage and said, 'I think – I think we have to keep going. We must rescue the pup's parents.'

Flax shook her head. 'A witch behind us and a dragon in front? And no magic? We can't possibly beat them. We *can't*...'

She hugged her little satchel. She nibbled the leather strap, and her voice dropped to a whisper, as if she was talking to herself. 'But if we don't, I can't go home. Not ever. And what about everyone else? What about Auntie Grub and Uncle Beech and Bean and Violet...They must be so scared.'

At last she swallowed and looked up. 'We have to do it. We have to get the Floating Forest back.'

'You're all mad,' the cake tin said bitterly. 'But I suppose you're going to take me with you whether I like it or not. Sheathe me, minch-wiggin, so I can pretend I don't know you.'

And with a grunt of effort, it turned back into a sword.

CHAPTER 38
Mount Tangle

They climbed up through the foothills.

Then they climbed higher. And higher.

The trees grew smaller. The rocks grew bigger.

The dragon drew closer...

Every time Flax thought about where they were going, she wanted to turn back. She wanted to hurry down the mountain as fast as she could. She wanted to *fall* down the mountain, if that was the quickest way to get there.

But somewhere in the clouds above her was the Floating Forest.

She could feel it in the tips of her whiskers, and when the wind turned, she could smell the leaves and bark. Once, she thought she heard the distant moan of a horned glob.

Home. It was the only thing that kept her going.

'How much – further?' panted Rose.

'I think it's quite a way yet,' said Flax. (She *hoped* it was quite a way. Because she had no idea how they were going to get the Floating Forest back from the dragon without any magic whatsoever.)

'Can we – stop for a bit?' asked Rose, plonking herself down on a boulder. 'To catch – our breath?'

The pup was some distance ahead of them. But he leapt back down, as bouncy as ever. 'Why are we stopping?'

'For a rest,' said Rose. 'Pup, when your parents were taken, did you actually see the dragon?'

'No,' said the pup.

'Then are you sure it *was* a dragon?' asked Rose. 'Might it have been the Lady?'

'Shhhh!' hissed Flax.

'Sorry,' whispered Rose. 'But could it have been *her*?'

The pup tipped his head to one side. 'I don't think so. I smelled the scorching and heard the growl. And if it was her, then she has my parents. Why would she still be trying to catch me?'

'Besides,' said Flax, 'we saw the dragon stealing the Floating Forest.'

'Might they have been working together?' asked Rose.

'I don't know,' said Flax. She drew the sword from its sheath. 'Sword? Could the L— Could the person you told us about have been working with the dragon?'

The sword sighed. 'I was in the middle of a very nice nap. Why did you wake me up with a foolish question?'

'Why is it foolish?' asked Rose.

'Dragons and witches hate each other,' said the sword. 'You are as likely to find me working with a soldier. Now, can I go back to sleep?'

Rose didn't look at all satisfied. 'But if *that person* didn't steal the pup's parents, how did she even know about him? How did she know he was here in Hallow?'

It was a good question. 'Maybe she saw him,' said Flax, 'when the *can't-see-us* wore off. Or maybe someone else saw him, and told her.'

The pup nosed her. 'Is there anything to eat?'

Before they started up the mountain, Flax had taken all the useless moss out of her satchel, and replaced it with a week's worth of acorns and thistles.

But a week's worth of food for a minch-wiggin is only a couple of mouthfuls for a hungry Spellhound pup. And when there's a human girl as well...

'Nothing,' said Flax.

The pup's ears drooped. 'Nothing at all?'

'Nothing at all. Look.' Flax turned her satchel upside down and shook it.

A tiny silver thread dropped out onto the rock and began to drift away.

A tiny silver thread of *magic*.

'Catch it!' squeaked Flax.

Rose and the pup dived after it at the same time. Rose almost had it, but it slipped through her fingers. The pup lunged past her – and caught the thread in his jaws.

'Ot it,' he mumbled, keeping his mouth closed. 'Ot ill I oo ith it?'

Flax scrambled over to him, her heart beating fast. 'When I say so, open your mouth really slowly. No, not yet...'

She put her cupped hands next to the pup's jaw. 'Now,' she whispered.

The pup's lip curled, and something gleamed from underneath it. Flax held her breath.

The pup's teeth separated – and the thread flew out.

But this time, Flax was ready. She grabbed it and held it tight. It wriggled for a moment, then grew still.

Flax tucked it back into her satchel and closed her eyes with relief. 'It must've been hiding in one of the seams. But now we've got it. We've got some magic. We've got a *chance*!'

Do you know the expression 'a hollow laugh'?

It is the way you laugh when something is not at all funny.

It is a laugh filled with sadness.

Or despair.

The sort of sound a prisoner might make if he learnt that a minch-wiggin was climbing Mount Tangle, armed with nothing but a talking sword and a single thread of magic.

And that she thought she had a *chance*.

Ha.

Ha.

Ha.

CHAPTER 39
The Darkness of the Mountain

The clouds cleared just after sunrise. And now at last Flax could see the Floating Forest, stuck on the topmost peak of Mount Tangle like a marshmallow on a stick, ready for toasting.

What? Yes, of course minch-wiggins eat toasted marshmallows. Who do you think invented them? It certainly wasn't humans.

Flax's heart thumped wildly, and she began to scramble up the mountain as fast as she could, desperate to see her beloved trees, which were full of magic from root to twig. Desperate to make sure that her cousins and aunties and uncles were unharmed.

She clambered over a slab of stone with a few stunted trees growing beside it. She trotted between two rocks, tall and forbidding—

And there, right in front of her was a tunnel entrance. There was another one to her right, and a third to her left.

All three led into the darkness of the mountain.

Flax stopped dead. 'The labyrinth,' she breathed.

She looked back at Rose, who was human, and therefore enormous. But next to the tunnels, she seemed terribly small.

So did the pup.

Flax had known that the dragon was big; she had seen it towing the Floating Forest across the sky.

But that was at a distance. Standing here, close

to where it lived, was a different matter altogether. Did it need every inch of these monstrous tunnels? Did its scaly back scrape against the roof when it went in and out? Did its wings brush the walls?

A single thread of magic isn't going to be nearly enough, she thought. *I'd need a satchelful. And even then—*

For the first time it struck her that defeating the dragon was not her only problem. Because even if she *could* beat it (which she definitely couldn't), how was she supposed to get the Floating Forest back to where it belonged?

She couldn't tow it. But neither could she leave it here, where an adventurous human might stumble upon it.

Her head spun, and if she had been by herself, she might have given in to fear and despair.

But the pup was pushing past her, sniffing at the left-hand tunnel.

His ears pricked. His tail wagged. 'My mother!' he said. 'My father! They're here!'

Flax blinked at him in astonishment. Through-

out their journey, she had never really believed
they'd find the pup's parents.

She was here for the Floating Forest, not the
Spellhounds. But the pup had been right all along.

'They're *alive*?' she asked, just to be sure.

The pup's tail wagged harder. 'Yes!'

Flax thought he was going to bolt straight into

the mountain. And she and Rose would have to run after him.

But he held himself back, even though his nose kept turning towards the left-hand tunnel.

Rose was as pale as a grub. She put her hand on one of the rocks, as if to steady herself. 'Is there anyone else in there? Anyone – human?'

The pup sniffed again. 'There's a faint smell like rotting eggs. I don't know what it is. But there's another smell, a *scorching*—'

His ears flattened and the hair on his back stood up in spikes. 'That's the smell from our den. That's the dragon!'

Eeeek! Flax clutched her satchel and sword. A sensible minch-wiggin would turn around *right now* and scramble back down the mountain.

But the pup's parents were alive, and that changed everything.

They can help me fight the dragon, she thought. *And – and maybe they'll know how to get the Floating Forest back where it belongs!*

She took a deep breath. 'We need a plan,' she whispered.

It was too hard to think with those huge tunnels looming over them, and the terrible darkness of the mountain. So in the end, they went back to the stone slab.

And there they huddled, like mice when the mor-kits are hunting.

'The plan is,' said Flax. 'The plan is—'

She drew the sword, to give herself courage. 'The plan is—'

'Another interrupted nap,' grumbled the sword. 'Where are we now?'

'On Mount Tangle,' said Flax. 'Near the laby-rinth. We're just trying to work out—'

'Mount *Tangle*?' croaked the sword. 'The *laby-rinth*? Nooooooo!'

And Flax found herself holding a belt buckle.

Rose gulped. 'We mustn't hang about for too long. We need to be quick.'

Flax nodded. Suddenly things were clearer.

'Is the dragon in there right now?' she asked the pup.

He tilted his head to one side, thinking. 'The dragon smell was a leftover smell. Not a *now* smell.'

Rose leaned forward. 'So it's not in there?'

'No,' said the pup.

'Maybe it's off stealing someone else's parents,' said Flax. 'Or someone else's home.' She swallowed. 'Maybe we should rescue your parents, pup, before it comes back.'

The pup's tail wagged once. Rose gave a very small nod.

Flaxseed, Destroyer-of-Dragons-and-Protector-of-her-People, gripped the belt buckle.

She stood up.

She led the way back to the labyrinth entrance.

The three of them crept into the mountain.

Spellhounds have amazing noses.

They can smell a storm from a hundred miles away. They can smell yesterday and the day before, and the day before that.

Sometimes they can even smell tomorrow.

But there are rare occasions when a Spellhound's nose is wrong.

Usually when there is a dragon involved...

CHAPTER 40
The Pup's Amazing Nose

The inside of Mount Tangle was riddled with tunnels. Some of them were as tall and wide as the entrance. Some were so narrow that the pup had to wriggle and squeeze to get through.

Their only light was the glow of Flax's whiskers, and the sparks struck by her feet.

Their only guide was the pup's amazing nose.

There were dead ends in those tunnels. And crevasses. And iron spikes set in the walls.

There were spiders. And snakes with wide, flat heads and blind eyes. And scorpions, as dark and dangerous as a witch's soul.

Yes, this part of the story *is* frightening.

But there is worse to come.

Do you want to turn back? Or will you gather your courage and keep going, like Flax, Rose and the pup?

You'll keep going?

Good.

The pup led Rose and Flax safely past every danger. And suddenly there was light ahead of them, where the tunnel opened up into an enormous cavern.

Flax stopped. So did Rose. The pup didn't, not until Flax whispered, 'Wait!'

The light was dim and green, as if they were underwater. Flax could hear the rumble of voices.

'Is that your parents?' she whispered to the pup.

'Yes!' he whispered in return.

Except it wasn't really a whisper.

It was more of a shout. An *excited* shout. A shout that carried all the joy of, *I've been looking everywhere for you, and HERE YOU ARE!*

There came a shout of disbelief in return. 'My *child*?'

That was enough for the pup. He bolted into the cavern, crying, 'Yes, it's *me*! I'm here. I've found you!'

Flax and Rose raced after him, hissing, 'Stop. Wait. Be careful.'

But the pup had forgotten everything except his parents.

Flax found him pressed up against close-set iron bars, trying to wriggle between them. On the other side of the bars were the missing Spellhounds.

In the Floating Forest, they had always seemed huge and glossy and powerful beyond belief. Now their black coats were dull and matted. Their ribs showed, and around their necks they wore iron bands.

They licked the pup's nose through the bars. They licked his ears and his eyes, and started on his nose again.

'How did you find us?' demanded his mother, in between licks. 'You shouldn't be here. You must go immediately.'

'Why did you come after us?' asked his father, pawing at the bars in frustration. 'Run away, my son. Run away now.'

'I'm not going,' said the pup. 'Not without you.'

'We're here to rescue you from the dragon,' said Rose.

'Felicia?' said an entirely new voice. 'Is that *you*?'

That's when Flax realised there were two other cells in the cavern. The door of the first one was open, and it looked more like a comfortable room than a cell.

The second one held a human man.

His hair was red, his body was thin and his clothes were ragged. Like the Spellhounds, he wore an iron band around his neck.

'Who—' said Rose.

'You don't know me?' said the man. 'Of course you don't; you were so young when I was taken. But you look just like your mother when she was your age. Felicia, I am your Uncle Edwin.'

CHAPTER 41
Vanished

Flax stared at the man. Who was Uncle Edwin? And why was he calling Rose 'Felicia'?

'Uncle *Edwin*?' whispered Rose. 'I thought you were dead. Everyone thought you were dead. Your portrait hangs in the place of honour behind the throne, next to my parents'.'

Throne? thought Flax. *What throne?*

'As you can see, I am alive,' said the man. 'But the Spellhounds are right, you must leave before—'

Something strange happened then. The man kept talking, but his words vanished before they reached Flax's ears.

It was as if the air had swallowed them in one big gulp.

Rose didn't seem to notice. 'Before the dragon comes back. We know. But we're not going without you. This is so amazing!'

She peered hopefully around the cavern. 'Is there anyone else here? Like – like my parents?'

The man shook his head.

'Oh' said Rose. 'Oh well. I didn't really think— Did the dragon steal you, Uncle Edwin?'

The man tried to say something else. 'It was—'

But his words vanished again.

The ends of Flax's whiskers prickled. 'It's magic, isn't it? There are things you can't say.'

Uncle Edwin nodded. 'But this I *can* say. You must go immediately.'

'Not without you,' said Rose.

'Not without my parents,' said the pup from the other side of the cavern.

'You do not understand,' growled his mother. 'You do not know the danger.'

'Yes we do,' said Rose. She turned to Flax. 'Can you unlock the doors? Quickly, before the dragon comes?'

The pup's father tried to say something. 'Before—'

But *his* words were swallowed by the air, too.

Flax stroked the belt buckle with trembling fingers. 'Will you be a key for us? As quick as you can?'

The belt buckle grumbled, but it was already changing shape.

Flax dashed across the cavern to the cell that held the Spellhounds.

'Aren't you going to free Uncle Edwin?' cried Rose.

'Spellhounds first, then him,' said Flax.

She held the key above her head so it could see the lock—

Yes, I *know* a key does not have eyes, any more than a sword has a throat and a mouth.

But are you seriously going to interrupt me *now*?

She held the key above her head so it could see the lock. Bits of the key grew bigger. Other bits grew smaller.

Rose ran across the cavern. 'Do you want me to turn it? It's an awfully big lock.'

Flax handed her the key, and Rose slid it into the keyhole.

It fitted perfectly.

The Spellhounds were watching. On the other side of the cavern, Uncle Edwin's eyes were round with hope.

Rose turned the key.

CHAPTER 42
Mouldy Horse Droppings

Nothing happened.

The lock did not click.

The barred door did not open, though Rose turned the key again and again.

Flax's heart sank.

'What's the matter?' asked the pup, nearly treading on Flax in his impatience. 'Why won't it open? Huh? Huh?'

'I don't know.' Rose pulled the key out of the lock. 'Key? Why isn't it opening?'

'Magic,' muttered the key. 'It smells like mould. Or horse droppings. Or *mouldy* horse droppings.'

'No,' whispered Rose. 'I don't believe it.'

She dashed across the cavern to the cell that held her uncle. She thrust the key into the lock.

She turned it.

And turned it.

And turned it.

'It's horrible in here,' said the key in a muffled voice, 'and it's not doing any good. You might as well give up.'

Behind the bars, Uncle Edwin sank to the floor with his head in his hands. 'Go,' he mumbled. 'Go, niece, before you too are captured.'

On the other side of the cavern, the pup's ears drooped. 'We can't open the doors? We can't rescue my parents? NooooOOOOOOooooo—'

'Be quiet,' snapped his mother. 'The—'

Flax knew what she meant to say. 'The dragon might hear you.' But the air swallowed her words, just as it had swallowed Uncle Edwin's.

They can't even say 'dragon', thought Flax. *That's how powerful it is.*

The key was right; they should give up.

Except—

'The thread of magic!' she squeaked.

She fumbled her satchel open, and seized the thread. She turned to the Spellhounds.

'It's only small. But if you called a thunderstorm, you could make it bigger!'

The pup's father tried to say something, but his words were lost. He shook his head and tried again. 'We cannot call a storm. Not without permission. Because of the—'

His hind leg came up and scratched helplessly at the band around his neck.

'Because of the collars?' asked Flax.

'Yes,' said the father. 'They stop us.'

'But our son does not wear a collar,' said the pup's mother, raising her head. 'He has never yet called a storm, and he is still very young. But he has seen us do it.'

The pup blinked. 'Call a storm? Me?'

His father nudged him through the bars. 'This is what you were born for. I would rather you had learnt in the forest, but we have no choice. Will you do it?'

'Uh,' said the pup.

'Of course he will,' said Rose. 'Quickly, before the dragon comes.'

'Uh,' said the pup.

'Wait,' whispered Flax. She had heard something.

The mountain was full of strange sounds. The clicking of beetles. The snap of scorpions.

But this was different. This was *arrival*.

Flax's heart beat much too fast. 'Someone has come into the labyrinth,' she whispered. 'Someone – or some*thing*.'

Rose's uncle Edwin jolted, as if he had been struck. His face reddened. He gripped the bars of his cell with both hands.

'You must get out of here,' he hissed. 'Now!'

He tried to say something else, but the words vanished from his mouth.

'We're going,' whispered Flax.

'But we'll be back,' said the pup.

'No!' said his mother. 'Go far.'

'Don't come back,' said his father, 'because—'
His words vanished, too.

'Quick,' Flax said to Rose. 'We've got to go.'

Rose didn't move.

'Hurry!' hissed Flax.

But Rose was staring at her uncle's hands, where they gripped the bars.

'Uncle Edwin,' she whispered. 'You've got *scales*!'

CHAPTER 43
You Did Not Realise...

The child was right. The backs of my hands were covered with red scales.

And my fingers did not end in fingernails. They ended in claws.

Yes, *my* hands. *My* fingers.

My claws.

What, all this time, and you did not realise you were talking to a dragon?

Dear me. Perhaps I forgot to mention it.

But you know now. So what are you going to do about it? Hmm?

Run away?

Scream?

Hide?

Oh, you're going to stay and listen to the rest of the story?

How brave you are.

Remember to sit very still, and have the green jellybabies at the ready.

In case I lose my temper...

CHAPTER 44
You're a Dragon

'You're a dragon,' whispered Rose. 'You look like a man, but you're not. You're a *dragon*.'

'Yes,' said her uncle. 'But there is something more important to worry about. You must watch out for— You must beware of—'

The words vanished from his mouth, and he shook his head in desperation.

'Felicia—' He made a great effort, and managed to croak, 'Felicia, don't *eat* anything.'

'You're a *dragon*,' Rose said again. And she turned and ran, with Flax and the pup racing after her.

But as soon as they were away from the light of the cavern, they had to slow down for fear of bumping headfirst into rock. Or something worse.

'I don't understand,' whispered Rose as they crept along. 'He's my uncle. His portrait hangs behind the throne, next to my parents'. How can he be a dragon? How *can* he?'

Flax didn't understand it either. But right now she was far more frightened about someone coming towards them through the labyrinth.

'Pup,' she whispered, 'can you smell scorching?'

'Not *new* scorching,' he rumbled. 'I think it might be a human.'

Rose stopped dead. 'You mean it's not another dragon? Then why are we trying to get away from them?'

'Because we don't know who it is,' hissed Flax. 'Here, go down *this* tunnel. No, not that one. The second one.'

They crept down the second tunnel. They turned left several times, then right again. Each time they came to a corner, Flax stopped and listened.

At last her heart slowed a little. 'I think we've lost them.'

'But what if they're here to help?' whispered Rose.

'What if they aren't?' Flax said grimly. 'Can you hear them, pup?'

'No,' said the pup. 'Have they gone? Can we go back to my parents now?'

Flax shook her head. 'They're still here somewhere. I think we should go outside and hide until they leave. Can you find the way out?'

'I think so,' said the pup.

He led them in silence through the dark, dangerous tunnels. Every now and then, they stopped so Flax could listen.

The first and second time, she heard nothing except the sounds of the mountain. The scuttle of scorpions. The drip of water. The *creak creak* of the rock above their heads.

The third time, she heard footsteps directly ahead of them.

It was too late to run. Flax gripped the belt buckle (which was now a toasting fork).

A light shone in their faces.

A dark shape loomed up behind it.

'Felicia,' said a pleased voice. 'I have found you at last.'

Rose gasped. 'Aunt Delilah!'

CHAPTER 45
Aunt Delilah

'But what—' said Rose. 'Why— How—'

Aunt Delilah swept towards them with her electric torch lighting up the tunnel. 'Such a relief, child. I did not want to start a panic, so I put out a proclamation that you were visiting your old nursemaid in the countryside. Meanwhile I have been turning Hallow upside down to find you. Are you all right? Are you injured?'

Her eyes fell on the pup, and she frowned. 'I hope that beast does not bite. And this is – what *is* this? Some sort of…pixie? And it has a little toasting fork. How quaint. Did these creatures kidnap you, Felicia? I cannot imagine how else you would be in their company.'

'They're my friends,' said Rose.

'Don't be ridiculous,' said Aunt Delilah. Now tell me, what are you doing in these dreadful tunnels?'

And suddenly Rose was sure that everything was going to be all right. Aunt Delilah might be bossy and bad-tempered, but she was an adult, and she wasn't afraid of anything. She would know what to do.

'It's the dragon, Aunt,' she said. 'It stole the pup's parents. And it stole the Floating Forest, too. That's why Flax is here. And – and *Uncle Edwin* is here! We thought he was dead, but he's not. And *he's* a dragon, too, at least I think he is. Except he's locked up, so I really don't understand what's happening.'

Aunt Delilah's eyes widened. 'Edwin is *alive*? The Duke of Spurr? And he is a *dragon*?'

'He's got red scales on his hands,' said Rose. 'And claws.'

'I have heard that some dragons can take human

form.' Aunt Delilah frowned again. 'But I never suspected it of Edwin Spurr. I hope you did not try to release him.'

Rose would have told her about Flax's toasting fork, which was really a sword but could also be a key if you asked politely.

But Flax pinched her ankle, as if the sword was a secret she didn't want to share.

Rose understood about secrets. So she simply said, 'We tried. But we couldn't. Now we don't know what to do. We thought you were *another* dragon coming...'

Aunt Delilah's face was grim. 'It is just as well I am not. We must—'

She broke off. 'Did you hear a noise?'

'What?' whispered Rose.

'Beetles,' said Flax.

Aunt Delilah ignored her. 'Something moved. Near the entrance to the labyrinth. Could it be the other dragon?'

Ice-water scorched through Rose's veins. Yes,

the dragon she had seen flying overhead was beautiful. Yes, she wanted to ask it if it had stolen her parents.

But she wanted to ask it from a safe distance.

Not when she was trapped inside a mountain.

'We have to get out of here,' she breathed.

'I can't smell it,' said the pup. It was the first time he'd spoken since Aunt Delilah appeared. 'Not a *now* dragon.'

Aunt Delilah shone her torch in his face. 'Do you doubt my word, dog?' she demanded, in the sort of voice that made visiting prime ministers quail. 'Of course there is a dragon. We will hide until it leaves again. Come with me. Quickly now, all of you.'

She strode away, and Rose picked up Flax and hurried after her aunt.

Close behind them, the pup said, 'I can't smell a *now* dragon, I really can't. I think we should stop.'

But Rose knew they *mustn't* stop. Not when her aunt used that tone of voice.

They hurried down one tunnel after another, with Aunt Delilah urging them on. 'Quickly now! We must not be caught by the dragon.'

On Rose's shoulder, Flax whispered, 'I can't hear—'

'*Hurry!*' hissed Aunt Delilah. 'We are nearly there.'

They rounded a corner. And suddenly the torch snapped off, leaving them in utter darkness.

Rose felt someone move past her. 'Aunt?' she whispered. 'Is that you? What are you doing?'

'I am making sure the dragon is not coming,' whispered her aunt from somewhere behind them. 'You keep going. Just a few steps more, and you will be safe.'

Rose took a step forward, running her hand along the rock.

'Rose!' whispered Flax. 'I can't hear your aunt's heartbeat!'

For one dreadful moment, Rose couldn't make sense of the words.

By the time she understood, it was too late.

There was a sudden smell of rotting eggs, and Aunt Delilah shouted, '𝔉𝔬𝔯𝔴𝔞𝔯𝔡!'

It wasn't just a word, like the ones Flax, Rose and the pup used.

It was a 𝔚𝔬𝔯𝔡.

And there was no standing against it.

The pup yelped with shock and terror, and bumped into Rose. She staggered, trying not to drop Flax – and some great force shoved the three of them forward in a scrabble of arms and legs, paws and tails.

Behind them, a door clanged shut.

A door made of bars.

Rose lay on the ground with her whole world crumbling around her.

'You're a witch, Aunt Delilah.'

But then an even worse thought struck her.

'You're the Lady!'

CHAPTER 46
Some Witches

Some witches will try to persuade you that not having a heartbeat is quite normal.

They will tell you that *you* are the strange one.

They will ask if you have a frog in your chest, hopping up and down. Or a clock, ticking away the hours.

They will pretend to pity you, because a heartbeat makes you weak.

Do not be fooled. They are jealous.

In their pursuit of power, they have given up kinship and kindness, friendship and feelings.

They have given up love.

But power cannot hug them when they are sad.

It cannot rejoice at the song of a blackbird, or gaze in awe at the beauty of a sunset. It cannot play or have fun.

If a witch tells you they are happy, do not listen to them.

They have forgotten what happiness is.

CHAPTER 47
The Lady

The torch snapped on again.

The witch who stood on the other side of the bars was tall and grey-faced. Her eyes reminded Flax of mid-winter, when the trees in the Floating Forest sometimes cracked under the weight of ice.

Her long sleeves covered her elbows.

Flax made herself very small, and hoped those wintry eyes wouldn't turn towards her. The toasting fork trembled in her hand.

'You are correct, Felicia,' said the witch. 'I am the Lady. But if you believe that is a bad thing, you are entirely wrong. My power protects Hallow from the dragon who calls himself

Edwin Spurr. If I had not imprisoned him, the whole country would be a blackened ruin. You would no longer be Queen, because there would be nothing left to be Queen *of.*'

Queen? thought Flax, staring at Rose. *QUEEN?*

Rose swallowed. 'But Aunt Delilah. You – you tricked us. You locked us up.'

'For your own good. Edwin Spurr is more dangerous than you can imagine, and I do not want you anywhere near him.'

'Is he the dragon that took my parents?' asked Rose.

'He is,' said the Lady.

'But *why* did he take them?' asked Rose.

'Why do dragons do anything?' said the Lady. 'Because they are vicious creatures who care for no one but themselves.'

A witch calling a dragon vicious?

A witch claiming that a *dragon* cares for no one but himself?

Ha.

We dragons are completely trustworthy.

Except when we are not.

The Lady hung the torch on the wall and turned away.

'Wait,' cried Rose. 'Aunt Delilah, I won't go near Uncle Edwin. Not now that I know what he is. So you could let me out. And my friends.'

'Your subjects,' said the Lady. 'Remember who you are.'

She turned away again, saying over her shoulder, 'I will release you soon, Felicia.'

'All of us? The pup's parents, too?'

'Of course. But for now this is the safest place for you.'

And she walked into the darkness.

Flax breathed out very quietly. 'You're the Queen,' she whispered. 'The Queen of Hallow.'

Rose looked at the floor.

'Your name isn't even Rose.'

'It's *one* of my names. And I've always liked it better than Felicia. I *feel* like Rose. So I didn't lie.'

'Yes you did,' whispered Flax. 'You told us you were a quite unimportant fourth chambermaid.'

'You wouldn't have taken me with you if you knew I was Queen. And I wanted to go so badly.'

The pup nosed her shoe. 'Your uncle is a dragon. Your aunt is the Lady. And you didn't tell us.'

'I didn't know,' cried Rose.

'Shh,' whispered Flax. 'Keep your voice down. What do we do now?'

'I suppose we wait for Aunt Delilah to let us out.'

The pup growled under his breath. 'She will not. She is the Lady. She has imprisoned my parents.'

'You said it was a dragon that stole them,' whispered Rose. 'Not a witch.'

'It doesn't matter who stole them,' hissed Flax. 'A witch has them now. The most dangerous witch of all.'

'But she said it was for our own good. She said this is the safest place for us.'

The toasting fork twitched in Flax's hand. 'If the Lady told me the world was round, I would know it was square. If she told me I was a mouse, I would suspect I was an elephant. If she told me the sun was high in the sky, I would look for it near the horizon.'

'Oh dear,' said Rose. 'I suppose you're right. In that case, we'd better try to escape.'

CHAPTER 48
If You Call a Thunderstorm

They huddled together and spoke in low voices so the witch would not hear them.

'Where's the Lady now, pup?' whispered Flax.

The pup sniffed the air. 'She is several tunnels away.'

'Do you think the room next to Uncle Edwin was hers?' asked Rose. 'There was a desk, wasn't there? And lots of papers? I'm sure there were papers.'

'As long as she's not nearby,' said Flax. 'If you call a thunderstorm, pup, we might be able to use my last thread of magic to escape. You can call it from in here, can't you?'

'I – I think so,' said the pup. 'But we should try the key first.'

Rose shook her head. 'We tried the key. It didn't work.'

'It didn't work in *those* doors,' said the pup. 'But it might work in this one.'

He's right, thought Flax. And she whispered to the toasting fork, 'Will you be a key again?'

'It's no use,' said the toasting fork. 'I can smell the magic from here.'

'Could you just try?'

'Do I ask *you* to go around sticking your nose into mouldy horse droppings? No, it's always me,' grumbled the toasting fork. (But now it was a key.) 'Well? What are you waiting for? Let's get it over with.'

Rose poked the key into the keyhole. It wriggled a bit, getting the shape right. Then it said in a muffled voice, 'Ugh, this is horrible. Turn me quickly. Though I'm telling you it won't do you any good.'

Rose turned the key.

And turned it.

'Told you so,' said the key. 'Now get me out of here. It's disgusting.'

And as soon as Rose drew it out of the lock, it became a toasting fork again.

'Right,' whispered Flax. 'We definitely need a thunderstorm, pup.'

She looked around the small cell. There wasn't much to it. Just a bed attached to the wall, and a chair, and a bucket in the corner.

'Do you know what to do?' she asked.

'I – I think so,' said the pup.

His ears were flat. His tail was tucked between his legs.

'I'm sure you can do it,' Rose said softly.

The pup licked his lips and braced himself. He raised his head...

'Wait!' whispered Flax. 'I hear footsteps. The Lady's coming back.'

CHAPTER 49
My Uncle is a Dragon

Rose wanted to laugh.

Not because any of this was the least bit funny, but because it was strange and terrible and wrong.

My uncle is a dragon, she thought. *My aunt is a witch. I wonder if I'm a – a goblin. Or a troll!*

That made her want to laugh even more. She let out a muffled squeak, and Flax whispered in her ear, 'Shh. She's got the Spellhounds with her.'

And suddenly Rose didn't feel like laughing.

Aunt Delilah strolled up to the bars of the cell with a different torch in her hand. She looked pleased with herself.

The Spellhounds didn't.

They sagged and limped. And when they saw their pup behind bars, they sagged and limped even more.

'You see?' said Rose's aunt. 'He is unharmed. And he will continue to be unharmed...as long as you do my bidding.'

The pup crept towards the bars. 'Mother?' he whined. 'Father?'

They looked at him but said nothing.

'So, do we have an agreement?' asked Aunt Delilah.

The Spellhounds' noses almost touched the ground.

'Yes,' said the pup's mother.

'Yes,' said his father.

'Um – Aunt Delilah?' said Rose. 'What are you doing?'

'I am making Hallow safer,' said her aunt. 'Now be quiet, Felicia. Practise your deportment. If you are very good, I will bring you cake.'

To the Spellhounds, she said, 'Come.' And she walked away.

They followed her. But just before they disappeared into one of the tunnels, the pup's father looked back over his shoulder and fixed his eyes on Flax.

'I am sorry,' he said.

Then he followed the Lady down the tunnel and out of sight.

Ah, the Spellhounds.

Such gallant creatures.

Despite the iron collars, they had held out against the Lady for days.

They could not harm her or escape from her. But they had refused to bow to her demands.

They had refused her bribes. They had refused her food.

But now she had them. How could they disobey when she held their pup's life in her hands?

CHAPTER 50
Why Did Your Father Apologise?

The pup was shivering.

He had never seen his parents so weak and helpless.

It made *him* feel weak and helpless, too.

He wished they were back in the Floating Forest, in their den. All curled up together in a warm heap.

He wished he had never heard of the Lady. And that *she* had never heard of Spellhounds.

Beside him, Flax whispered, 'Why did your father apologise, pup?'

'I don't know,' said the pup.

'Aunt Delilah was threatening them, wasn't she?'

said Rose. 'She was threatening to do something nasty to you if they didn't help her. Do you think she meant it?'

'She meant it,' said Flax.

Rose twisted her fingers together. 'I knew she was bossy and particular. And that she thought I wasn't a very good queen. But I didn't think she'd actually *hurt* anyone.'

'That's the Lady for you,' muttered the toasting fork. 'Lies and hurt. Hurt and lies. All mixed up with powerful magic.'

'Maybe my parents will get away from her,' said the pup. 'Maybe they'll attack her.'

But he knew they wouldn't. Not while the Lady had him locked up and at her mercy.

'I wish we knew what she's going to do,' whispered Flax. 'Why does she need the Spell-hounds? Why does she need her magic to be even more powerful? It can't be good.'

They fell silent. The mountain creaked. The scorpions scuttled.

'I should have waited for a soldier after all,' mumbled the toasting fork. 'Oh why didn't I wait for a soldier?'

The pup sat up. Somewhere far away, a storm was brewing.

He couldn't see it. He couldn't hear it.

But he could smell it. And he could feel it, deep in his Spellhound bones. The rumble of thunder and the snap of lightning.

'My parents are calling a storm,' he said.

'Where is it?' asked Flax.

'A long way away.'

He tried his hardest not to move. But as the storm came closer, the hair on his back stood on end, and his teeth ground together.

'Where is it now?' whispered Flax.

'Right overhead.'

Flax's eyes lit up with sudden hope. 'Pup, could you call a bit of it down here, to strengthen my thread of magic? We might be able to escape before the Lady comes back.'

Rose put her hands over her mouth. 'And then we could find a way to rescue your parents.'

Rescue his parents? Was it possible? Inside his chest, the pup's heart zigzagged like lightning. The storm at the top of the mountain crackled and sparked, and some part of him crackled and sparked, too.

He braced his legs.

He braced his Spellhound heart and his Spellhound soul.

He called the edge of the storm.

CHAPTER 51
Crash and Sizzle

Thunder came rumbling down through the mountain, with a sound like ten thousand automobiles.

Lightning followed.

The cell was full of crash and sizzle, and the pup stood in the very middle of it.

For one glorious moment, Flax was sure it was going to work. The pup would take the power of the storm inside him, and she could use it to strengthen her last thread of magic.

They were going to escape!

But instead of eating the thunder and swallowing the lightning, as a Spellhound was supposed to do, the pup let out a yelp of terror – and dived under the bed.

The crash faded away.

The sizzle vanished.

Flax and Rose were left pressed against the wall of the cell, staring at the pup.

His paws were over his eyes, and his tail was jammed between his legs. He was trembling all over.

'Nooooooo,' he whimpered. 'I can't do it! Please don't make me!'

And so another Dark and Terrible Secret is revealed.

A Spellhound pup who is afraid of thunder and lightning.

There is, of course, nothing unusual about being afraid. Even dragons are afraid sometimes.

But a Spellhound who is afraid of storms is like a

fish who is afraid of swimming. Or a mor-kit who faints at the sight of blood.

I suppose there *are* such fish and such mor-kits, somewhere in the world. But perhaps their friends do not need them to swim and bite quite as desperately as Flax and Rose needed the pup to call the storm.

Ah well. At least we have reached the lowest point of our story.

After all, things couldn't possibly get worse.

Could they?

CHAPTER 52
Things Get Worse

When all the rumble and flash had vanished, Flax crawled under the bed and snuggled up next to the pup. She wrapped her small arms around his trembling paw.

Rose crept in beside them.

None of them spoke. Flax was remembering her satchel, and how ashamed she had felt when she had to confess its emptiness.

She tried to think of something wise she might say. Something that would make the pup feel better.

But she couldn't think of a single thing.

'Please don't tell my parents,' mumbled the pup.

'We won't.' Rose stroked his ear. 'You know what? I'm afraid of Aunt Delilah. And Uncle Edwin. And I'm afraid of spiders – the little scuttly ones that hide in your shoes. And I'm afraid of people realising I'm not a very good queen.'

The pup snuffled into his paws.

'I'm afraid of the World Below,' whispered Flax. 'And mor-kits and sketters, and ending up in soup. I'm afraid of the Lady. And I'm afraid of everyone finding out that I'm no good at being Destroyer-of-Dragons-and-Protector-of-her-People.'

'It's not the same,' mumbled the pup. 'You aren't afraid of climbing, are you?'

No, thought Flax. There wasn't a minch-wiggin in the world who was afraid of climbing. Minch-wiggins were *meant* to climb. Just as Spellhounds were meant to eat thunder and swallow lightning.

She snuggled closer to the pup, and sang quietly about blueberries and beechnuts, which comforted all of them, even though they were dreadfully hungry and afraid.

They slept for a little while, with the pup dribbling down Flax's neck.

Then they woke.

The Lady was coming back.

To Flax, still half asleep, the Lady's footsteps sounded...different.

She looked different too, when she appeared. She sagged almost as much as the Spellhounds. Her hair was in disarray. Her sleeves were torn, and the grey feathers on her elbows poked out.

She smelled of magic – the magic that Flax knew belonged to the trees in a certain part of the Floating Forest.

Only now it was hers.

Flax sat bolt upright, speechless with horror.

The Lady limped past their cell without stopping. The pup's mother and father followed her.

Flax's horror was reflected in their eyes.

As the Lady passed out of sight, the pup's father said hoarsely, 'She has ripped the magic from half the trees in Sketterhome. In the morning, she will

start on Minchfold. Destroyer-of-Dragons-and-
Protector-of-her-People, can't you—'

'Come, my little pets,' cried the Lady, from
further down the tunnel. 'It has been a tiring day
and I need to sleep.'

The Spellhounds went.

Flax, Rose and the pup clung to each other.
'She's stealing *magic*?' whispered Rose. 'But why?'

'To make herself more powerful,' whispered
Flax.

The pup whined, 'But the magic belongs to the
Floating Forest.'

'Not anymore,' whispered Flax. 'Now it's hers.'

What would the Floating Forest be without its
magic?

Just a forest, like any other.

That would be tragedy enough.

But there is another question, just as important.

What would Hallow be, without the Floating Forest?

Some people would see no difference. No difference at all.

But others would wonder why the stars shone less brightly.

Why birdsong was not as sweet.

Why Dashy Slove and Mansie Undercroft no longer smiled and laughed.

This is the Second Great Secret: the Floating Forest is the very heart of Hallow.

Without it, there is no joy.

CHAPTER 53
The Real *Griv*

This is the real griv, thought Flax. *It's disaster. It's end-of-the-world, and hide-little-minch-wiggin-hide, and don't-bother-hiding-because-nothing-can-save-you.*

The Floating Forest was going to lose its magic. And Flax couldn't do a thing to stop it.

Because the Lady was a witch. She was *the* witch. She had a hole where her heartbeat should be, and it was full of power and greed.

Whereas Flax was just a small, frightened minch-wiggin. A small, frightened, *imprisoned* minch-wiggin. She might as well give up.

And that's what she did.

They all gave up. Flax, Rose and the pup.

They huddled under the bed, feeling small and lost. Flax couldn't even bring herself to sing.

After a while, they slept again.

Flax dreamt of the Floating Forest. She dreamt of mossy paths and clear cold streams. Of vines and fern glades, and the early morning light filtering through the green leaves.

She dreamt of the deep, slow song of the ancient trees, which only a minch-wiggin could hear. And the magic that ran through everything, and made the forest what it was.

By the time she woke, she knew she *couldn't* give up. Because the Floating Forest was her home.

I'm supposed to be Destroyer-of-Dragons-and-Protector-of-her-People, she thought. *I'm supposed to stop* griv, *not just sit back and let it happen.*

But *how* could she stop it?

Or rather, how could the three of them stop it? Because the forest was the pup's home, too.

And Rose was their friend, even though she was human.

And Queen.

And had the worst possible relatives.

Flax crawled out from under the bed and began to trot in circles, with the toasting fork in her hand.

Small circles at first, then bigger and bigger.

Worrying and thinking.

After a while, Rose woke up and joined her.

Then the pup.

Round and round they went.

Worrying. And thinking.

And getting angry.

'The Lady's nasty,' said Flax. 'She's going to destroy the Floating Forest, and she's *pleased* about it.'

'She's greedy,' said the pup. 'If there were three horned globs, she'd eat them all and leave none for me.'

'She's already Regent,' muttered Rose. 'She's already the Lady. Why does she need more power? Why does she—'

Rose stopped, and put her hand on her

tummy. 'I feel strange,' she said. 'Fizzy. Like a firecracker—'

'Good morning, Felicia,' said the Lady, from the other side of the bars. 'I have brought your breakfast.'

All her tiredness and raggedness of the night before was gone. Her hair was smooth and so were her sleeves. She was sleek with stolen magic.

In her hands she carried a silver tray, with a large cream cake and a silver knife beside it. The two Spellhounds stood behind her.

It was one thing to be angry with the Lady when she was nowhere in sight. It was another thing entirely when she was right there in front of them.

The pup crept behind Rose. (Though he was so big that most of him poked out.)

Flax crept behind the pup.

The toasting fork became a very small thimble.

Rose stared at the ground. 'I would rather you released us, Aunt.'

'And so I will,' said the Lady. 'Very soon.'

With a **Word**, she unlocked the cell door and held out the tray. 'Say thank you, Felicia. A queen is *never* ungrateful.'

Rose took the tray. 'Thank you, Aunt,' she mumbled.

The Lady locked the door again. 'Now eat your breakfast. I have important work to do.'

And she strode towards the labyrinth entrance, with the Spellhounds following her.

As helpless as Flax.

CHAPTER 54
Cake

Rose put the cake on the bed and stared at it.

In her old life, there had been too much cake. But since she'd left the palace, there had not been nearly enough.

She reached for the silver knife.

'How can you think about cake at a time like this?' hissed Flax. 'The Lady's going to steal the magic from Minchfold!'

'And we can't do anything to stop her,' said Rose. 'I wish we could. But we can't.'

She reached for the knife again.

'Your uncle told you not to eat anything.'

'He didn't mean *cake*,' said Rose. 'He meant –

um, witchy potions. And besides, he's a dragon. He's not to be trusted.'

The thimble muttered, 'If the Lady told me someone was not to be trusted...'

Rose stared at it. 'You think we should trust a *dragon*?'

'In general, no,' said the thimble. 'But in these particular circumstances, yes.'

'But I'm hungry,' said Rose. 'And Aunt Delilah *told* me to eat it. If I don't, she'll be angry. She might decide not to let us out after all.'

'She's not going to let us out,' said Flax. 'She was lying.'

'But what if she wasn't?' said Rose.

The pup licked his lips. 'If *I* ate it, she'd think it was you.'

'But it's mine,' said Rose. 'It's *my* cake.'

And there was the fizzing in her tummy again.

'Why did she give it to you?' asked Flax.

'Because I'm *hungry*,' said Rose. 'I *told* you. Queens aren't *supposed* to get hungry.'

Flax looked at her uncertainly. 'Are you all right?'

'Of course I'm all right,' snapped Rose. Though really, she was feeling hot and angry. Like a firecracker. One of the ones that started off slowly . . .

'I just need to eat some cake.' And she picked up the knife.

'Wait!' cried Flax.

'What is it this time?' snapped Rose.

Flax held up the thimble. 'Can I cut it? Please?'

Rose rolled her eyes (which queens were not supposed to do). 'Hurry up, then.'

'Really?' cried the thimble. (Only now it was a cake knife.) 'Oh joy! What sort of slices would you like? Big or small? The traditional shape or something more innovative?'

'I don't care,' said Rose. 'Just do it.'

'You'll have to move,' said Flax. 'I don't want to cut you by mistake.'

Rose stepped away from the bed. The fizzing had spread out from her tummy and was racing down her legs.

It was the oddest feeling.

Flax held the cake knife over the cake. The pup drooled. The cake knife hummed with anticipation. 'The icing smells a bit strange,' it said. 'But *I* don't care either.'

It sliced downwards.

Once.

Twice.

The neatest piece of cake Rose had ever seen.

'That'll do,' she said.

'One more,' said Flax. 'Stand back.'

The cake knife dived into the cake again, then sighed happily. 'That was lovely. Apart from the icing.'

Rose reached for the nearest slice. But before she could get hold of it, Flax shouted, 'Pup, eat it!'

The pup lunged forward. His mouth closed over the slice Rose was reaching for.

No, his mouth closed over *the whole cake*.

He inhaled.

The cake vanished.

Rose felt as if she was going to explode. 'That was *my* cake! It was mine!'

The fizzing feeling raced down her arms and into her fingers.

I'm a firecracker, she thought. *One of the ones that start off slowly, so you think they're not going to be very interesting. But then they get big. And—*

'Rose,' squeaked Flax. 'Your hands!'

CHAPTER 55
Rose's Hands

Rose's hands were covered in red scales. Her fingernails were sharp and curved. Her face was a picture of bewilderment.

If the cell door had been open, Flax would have run out into the labyrinth and done her best to get lost. (Even though it was impossible for a minch-wiggin.)

But the door was closed and locked, and there was nowhere to run.

Flax looked around for the pup, but he was hiding under the bed again.

She swallowed. 'I – I think we should all just try to – to stay calm.'

'I don't feel calm,' said Rose.

But her voice was changing. It was deep and growly, like this: **'I DON'T FEEL CALM.'**

The pup hiccuped. Flax took a step backwards. With trembling hands, she raised the cake knife.

Only now it was a teaspoon.

'Are you *mad*?' hissed the teaspoon. 'Are you trying to get us killed?'

'I don't know what else to do,' whispered Flax.

'I suggest we hide under the bed,' said the teaspoon.

Flax dived under the bed, next to the pup, and they both trembled.

By now, Rose's ankles were covered in scales, too. **'A QUEEN DOES *NOT* GO BAREFOOT,'** she muttered. But she kicked off her shoes, and stomped around the cell on scaly feet.

Flax heard a ripping noise.

'OOPS,' muttered Rose. **'STUPID COAT.'**

Something thumped against the wall above the bed.

'OW,' said Rose. **'THIS CELL IS TOO SMALL.'**

Something scraped against the roof.

'AND THE CEILING'S TOO LOW!'

But then Rose fell silent.

It was not a small, comfortable silence. It was a big, puzzled silence.

Flax held her breath. So did the pup.

The silence came closer.

A long, scaly nose peered under the bed. Golden eyes blinked. A puff of steam escaped from cavernous nostrils.

'FLAX,' said Rose. **'AM I A DRAGON?'**

Did I know?

Of course I knew.

It is the First Great Secret.

That Felicia, our beloved Queen, is a dragon.

As was Alyss, her mother.

CHAPTER 56
A Scaly Tail

Flax managed to squeak, 'Y-yes. You're a d-dragon.'

'THAT'S WHAT I THOUGHT,' said Rose.

She stomped around the cell again. Flax glimpsed the edge of a wing. A long neck thrust through a torn coat. The end of a scaly tail.

The pup put his paws over his eyes.

'I DON'T LIKE THIS CELL,' said Rose.

She stomped over to the door. Her head tilted one way, then the other.

She stuck the tip of a claw into the lock, and pulled.

The door tore away from its hinges and fell to the ground with a clang.

'OOPS,' said Rose.

She picked up the door and tossed it to one side. Then she ducked her head and stomped out of the cell and along the tunnel.

Flax and the pup crept out from beneath the bed and followed her.

'Where's she going?' whispered Flax.

'I don't know,' said the pup. He hiccuped. 'I think there was something wrong with the icing, Flax. I think there was ^{hic} magic in it.'

She stopped. 'Will you be all right?'

'I expect so. Spellhounds can eat ^{hic} most things.'

Rose marched down the tunnel and around several corners. Flax and the pup hurried after her.

And there was the cavern with the other cells, and Uncle Edwin leaping to his feet with a cry of, 'Felicia!'

Rose stomped up to her uncle's cell door and hooked her claw into the lock.

Flax leapt forward in horror. 'No! No, Rose, he's a *dragon*!'

'**SO AM I,**' said Rose. And she tore the door off its hinges and tossed it away.

To Flax's relief, Uncle Edwin didn't immediately leap out of his cell and kill them all.

Instead, he sank onto his bed with his head in his hands. 'It is no use,' he said. 'While I wear this collar, I cannot step outside the cell. Not without permission from—'

The rest of his words vanished. Rose said, '**NOT WITHOUT PERMISSION FROM AUNT DELILAH?**'

Her uncle nodded.

Rose marched into his cell. She stuck her claws inside the iron collar and tried to wrench it apart. When that didn't work, she tried to bite it off, and nearly bit her uncle in the process.

'**AAARGH!**' she growled. '**WHY CAN'T I DO IT?**'

'It's magicked,' said the teaspoon. 'I can smell it from here.'

'Shh!' hissed Flax.

But she was too late. Rose stared at the teaspoon. **'IF YOU WERE A KEY, YOU COULD UNLOCK IT.'**

'Not a chance,' said the teaspoon. 'It'll be mouldy horse droppings all over again.'

'BUT IF FLAX USED HER LAST THREAD OF MAGIC...'

Flax clutched her satchel. 'No. Your uncle's a *dragon*, Rose. He's *dangerous*.'

'THAT'S THE POINT,' said Rose. **'MAYBE HE'S DANGEROUS ENOUGH TO STOP AUNT DELILAH.'**

She turned back to her uncle. **'COULD YOU STOP HER?'**

'I do not know,' he said. 'I have been her prisoner for so long. I *think* I could, but I am not sure.'

Rose stared at Flax across the cavern. **'SOON THE PUP'S PARENTS WILL CALL A STORM, AND AUNT DELILAH WILL STEAL THE MAGIC FROM YOUR HOME.'**

'I know,' whispered Flax.

'WE MUST STOP HER.'

Flax swallowed. With a shaking hand, she raised the teaspoon. 'If – if we used my last thread, could you unlock the collar?'

'It won't be enough,' said the teaspoon. 'The thread's too small and the magic's too strong.'

'Not,' said Flax, looking up at the pup, 'if we could make the thread bigger...'

CHAPTER 57
Don't Ask Me

The pup shrank back against the rock wall. Eat thunder? Swallow lightning? He had already tried once, and failed. If he tried again, he would fail again.

The mere thought of it made his legs shake.

'I can't,' he whispered. 'I can't, Flax. Please ^{hic} please don't ask me.'

Flax stroked his leg. 'You're our only hope. We need you, pup. The Floating Forest needs you. Your parents need you.'

The pup remembered the look of despair in his father's eyes. *'She has ripped the magic from half the trees in Sketterhome...'*

'Won't you try?' asked Flax.

The pup was shaking all over now. But the Floating Forest needed him. And so did his parents.

'W-will you ^{hic} stay with me?' he whispered.

Flax nodded. 'I will.'

'SO WILL I,' said the dragon who was Rose.

The pup took a deep breath.

He closed his eyes.

He called a storm.

It was like sending a part of himself up into the sky and far away. A very small, frightened part of himself. He could feel it up there, shivering.

And seeking.

He sent it further. Past the borders of Hallow and out across the mountains of Quill.

Past the mountains to the deserts.

And there, in the heat and the swirling air, he found a thunderstorm.

The small, frightened part of him wanted to yelp with terror and scuttle away. But Flax was leaning against his leg. Rose had wrapped her tail around both of them, like a big scaly hug.

And his parents needed him.

So the pup took another deep breath and sang to the storm. The way he had heard his parents sing.

A calling song, which no one but Spellhounds could hear.

A *come-to-me* song. With hiccups.

Then the small, *very* frightened part of him raced back to his body, and waited.

'Is it coming?' whispered Flax.

The pup couldn't see it. He couldn't hear it.

But he could smell it. And he could feel it, deep in his Spellhound bones.

The rumble of thunder. The snap of lightning.

'It's ^{hic} coming!'

CHAPTER 58
A Great Wound

I was not there when the witch set out to strip the magic from the trees of Minchfold.

Neither were Flax, Felicia or the pup.

But the pup's parents were. His mother, who is named She-Who-Will-Call-The-Tempest. And his father, His-Fury-Is-The-Blizzard.

This is what they told me.

Minchfold was usually a noisy, bustling town, full of noisy, bustling minch-wiggins.

But now it was deserted. The hammocks and

swings were silent, and so were the great trees.

The witch gazed up at them with a hungry expression. 'Call me a storm,' she demanded.

Yesterday had torn a great wound through the Floating Forest. It did not *look* as if it was bleeding. But the Spellhounds could feel it.

'Call a storm,' snarled the witch, 'or your pup will suffer.'

'We cannot' said His-Fury-Is-The-Blizzard. 'You took too much power from us yesterday.'

It was a lie, and the witch knew it. But before she could speak, both Spellhounds felt a storm being called.

It was their son.

They did not want the witch to know what the pup was doing. So She-Who-Will-Call-The-Tempest said, 'However, we will do our best.'

The two Spellhounds raised their heads and gazed into the distance.

They lent their strength to the pup.

They helped him call the storm.

CHAPTER 59
The Storm

Flax pressed herself against the pup's trembling flank.

She was trembling, too. What if this didn't work? What if the pup's hiccups stopped it somehow? What if he was too scared?

What if *she* was too scared?

After all, she had never actually seen a Spellhound eat thunder and swallow lightning. But now she thought about it, it sounded awfully dangerous.

Maybe she should hide under Uncle Edwin's bed, just in case. Or out in the labyrinth, where the thunder and lightning couldn't reach her.

But she had promised the pup she would stay with him.

'WHERE IS IT?' asked Rose. **'WHERE IS THE STORM?'**

'Overhead,' whispered the pup. He opened his eyes. 'And c-coming hic closer!'

The hair on his back stood up in a ridge. Flax could hear his teeth grinding.

And then she heard the storm.

No, she *felt* the storm.

It came crashing down through the mountain, through gaps and gullies, through caves and cracks, through soil and solid rock.

Thunder, a thousand times bigger and wilder than a dragon.

Lightning, as sharp and bright as the sun.

All of it pouring into the cavern, which suddenly felt much too small.

Flax put her hands over her ears and tried to burrow into the floor. Beside her, the pup and Rose were doing the same.

Where was I?

Hiding under the bed, of course.

I am a dragon, not a fool.

Eeek! thought Flax. *Eeeeeeeeeeeeeeeeeeeeeek!*

All around them the storm raged. It bounced off the rock walls. It set fire to the bed, driving Uncle Edwin out from under it.

'Spellhound!' he shouted, and Flax could barely hear him over the rumbling of the thunder, and the terrible spark of the lightning. 'Spellhound, you must control it or it will kill us all!'

The pup didn't move. Except perhaps to hiccup, and try even harder to burrow into the floor.

Flax grabbed hold of his ear with shaking hands. She shouted, 'Pup, we're here! Rose and me and the sword – I mean the teaspoon. We're here with you!'

She thought perhaps the pup whimpered,

though the sound was lost in the storm.

But then his ear twitched. Just a little.

'We're here!' Flax shouted again.

On the pup's other side, Rose cried, **'WE'RE WITH YOU.'**

For a moment, Flax thought they hadn't made any difference.

But then the pup opened his eyes, though they were white with terror.

He stood up, though his legs were trembling.

He braced himself.

He breathed in... and in... and in...

And suddenly the hiccups and the terror left him. He opened his mouth wider than Flax had thought possible – and **roared**.

It was the biggest sound Flax had ever heard him make. Her skin prickled all over. She could smell the lightning, as sharp as a hedgehog needle in her nose. She wanted to run, but she stayed.

The pup **roared** again. He snapped at the lightning with his great teeth. He bit the thunder in half and swallowed it. His eyes burned in his head; his paws scorched the ground.

He danced on the spot, full of crash and sizzle.

'Now,' he said, in a voice almost as big as Rose's. **'Try your magic now.'**

CHAPTER 60
The Echo and the Flash

Not *all* of the storm went down into the mountain.

She-Who-Will-Call-The-Tempest and His-Fury-Is-The-Blizzard had to eat some of it, to fool the witch.

So they snapped at the edges of it. They bit the echo instead of the thunder. They swallowed the flash instead of the lightning.

But they did it with such roaring, with such prancing and leaping, that anyone watching would have thought they had eaten the whole thing.

The Lady waited until they were done. Then she grabbed for their power.

And even though they had only eaten the echo and the flash, it was enough to make her stronger.

She raised her hands, ready to steal the magic from the trees of Minchfold.

One by one.

Deep inside the mountain, the cell was quiet. The whole cavern was quiet. All the thunder and lightning was inside the pup, and he was ablaze with it.

With trembling hands, Flax unfastened the buckle of her satchel. She took out the last tiny thread of magic.

She tied the most complicated knot she could think of. Then she untied it again. She leaned against the pup and held up the teaspoon, which was now a key.

She swallowed the thread.

'Whoa,' cried the key, twitching in her hand. 'This is different. Where's the collar? Let me at it.

Got anything else you want unlocked? A secret? A treasure chest? A closed heart?'

Uncle Edwin knelt before Flax. 'Minch-wiggin,' he said quietly. 'Free me, and everything I have is yours.'

His collar was still too far away for Flax to reach. So Rose picked her up.

Flax slipped the key into the little padlock.

'Yay,' cried the key. 'I can do this. Mouldy horse droppings, see if I care. Turn me. Go on, turn me!'

Flax didn't move. *I'm letting loose a dragon,* she thought. *Not a friendly dragon like Rose. An unknown dragon. The sort I'm supposed to destroy.*

She swallowed. She turned the key.

CHAPTER 61
Hungry

Have you ever worn shoes you could not take off, no matter how hard you tried?

Shoes that blistered your heels when you walked?

That left you helpless before your worst enemy?

No, of course you haven't.

But if you *had*, you might have some understanding of how I felt when that cursed collar fell from my neck.

Freedom, for the first time in eight years.

I was dizzy with it.

I was mad with it.

And I was hungry. She had not fed me well, the witch.

I looked at the little dragon. I could not eat my own niece.

Nor could I eat the Spellhound pup – he was too important.

But the minch-wiggin...

I almost reached for her. That was how far I was from honour. If I had been in my dragon form, I would have snapped her up without thinking. I would have killed the very person who had freed me.

But I stopped myself in time.

I breathed deeply. I remembered who I was and what I must do.

I led the way out of the labyrinth into the glorious sunlight.

I Changed.

CHAPTER 62
I am Not Strong Enough

Flax couldn't take her eyes off the dragon. This was the same terrifying creature who had towed the Floating Forest across the sky.

He had red-gold scales, and spikes all the way down his back to his tail. His eyes were scarlet and black. His teeth were as long as Flax was tall.

He was dreadfully thin.

She half expected him to eat her on the spot. Instead, he raised his head and growled, '**I CANNOT FACE THE WITCH YET; I AM NOT STRONG ENOUGH. DELAY HER, AND I WILL COME AS SOON AS I CAN.**'

He hunched his shoulders and spread his

wings. His claws scraped against the rock. He launched himself into the air and flew down the mountain.

Leaving Flax, Rose and the pup staring after him.

'I THOUGHT HE WAS SUPPOSED TO SAVE US,' said Rose.

'How can we delay a *witch*?' said Flax.

'Impossible,' muttered the key (which was a sword again). 'We'd need an army.'

'Well we haven't got an army,' snapped Flax. 'So we're going to have to think of something else—'

She broke off. She looked at the sword. She began to trot in a very small circle.

'What is it?' asked the pup.

Flax stopped, halfway around the circle. 'Rose, can you fly like your uncle? Could you fly us up to the Floating Forest?'

'I DON'T KNOW. I CAN TRY.'

Rose spread her wings cautiously. She flapped them twice. She left the ground— And fell back again.

'OW.'

She tried a second time, flapping harder. This time, she flew a little way before she fell in a heap.

The third time, she launched herself off the side of the mountain.

'Rose, no!' cried Flax.

'I can't watch,' said the pup. **'Tell me when it's over.'**

Rose fell and fell. Her wings flapped wildly. She tumbled head over heels towards the rocks below...

And then, somehow, she righted herself. The wind caught her wings and she raised her head.

She flew!

Up and up and up she soared. Her scales glittered in the morning sun. Her tail was like a bolt of lightning across the sky.

Then she swooped down so fast that Flax and the pup dived behind the nearest rock.

They heard a clatter and a crash.

'WHOOPS,' said Rose. **'I MIGHT HAVE TO PRACTISE LANDING.'**

Flax peeped around the side of the rock.

'DID YOU SEE ME FLY?' boomed Rose, looming above her. **'IT WAS AMAZING,**

FLAX. IT WAS EVEN BETTER THAN GREEN JELLYBABIES.'

'Um,' squeaked Flax. 'Could you not show so many teeth?'

'**I WAS SMILING,**' said Rose.

'I don't think dragons are supposed to smile,' squeaked Flax. 'Not unless they want to scare their friends.'

Rose's sharp teeth disappeared. '**SO WHOT HOPPENS NOO?**'

'Now,' said Flax, 'you fly us up to the Floating Forest.'

CHAPTER 63
The Floating Forest

Flax yelped with fright when Rose left the ground. The wind beat about her ears, and she clung to the pup and kept her eyes tightly shut until a jolt told her they had landed.

And there was the Floating Forest, all around her, mossy and green. There were the great trees towering so high that they hid most of the sky. There were the little paths, the rotting logs, the rocks and insects.

Flax slid from Rose's back, feeling better than she'd felt for days. Because she was home again.

Feeling *worse* than she'd felt for days. Because home was not the place it used to be.

Some of the magic that held the Floating Forest together was gone.

And in its place was fear.

Flax could feel it.

The trees were afraid. So were the horned globs. And the owls, and the little brown mice, and the bats and bees and minch-wiggins.

Even the sketters were frightened.

Even the mor-kits.

'What now?' asked the pup, leaping down beside her.

'Now you and Rose keep an eye on the witch,' said Flax. 'I'm going to fetch an army.'

And with that astonishing statement, she hurried away with her sword in her hand.

'Where are we going?' demanded the sword. 'And what's this about an army? I won't have anything to do with guns. I'm very sensitive to loud noises.'

'No guns,' said Flax.

But she refused to say anything more. Mainly

because she wasn't at all sure her plan would work.

Or that she would come out of it alive.

It is easy to be brave when you are a dragon.

But Flax, trotting through the Floating Forest, showed more courage than I ever have.

She was afraid, but she kept going. She thought she would probably end up dead, but she kept going.

Great strength does not lie in invasions and brute force.

It lies in the heart of a small, frightened minch-wiggin who loves her home.

CHAPTER 64
Sketterhome

Sketters lived in dens, like Spellhounds. But Spellhounds were clean, and sketters were...not.

Flax could smell Sketterhome from five hundred paces. At *five* paces, the stink was almost enough to kill her.

She held her nose and stared around in dismay.

Sketterhome was one of the thickest parts of the forest. (Which really helped with the smell.)

But now, more than half of its trees had lost their magic.

They stood empty and silent, like the trees in the World Below. All around them lay bare earth, bones, soup pots—

And two hundred sketters, big and small. All staring hungrily at Flax.

'So what's the plan?' whispered the sword.

'Um – I have to talk to them,' squeaked Flax. 'And they have to listen.'

Now she was here, she could see how unlikely that was.

The sketters were bristling with anger, hatred, despair, loss and misery, all mixed up together in a big, painful lump.

And they were looking for someone to take it out on.

'A minch-wiggin?' growled a huge sketter with blue beads in his ears. 'Here in Sketterhome? What does it want? Is it lost?'

'Not just *a* minch-wiggin,' growled a different sketter with a necklace of delicate finger-bones. 'It's the little Destroyer. I wonder what it tastes like.'

'I ate a Destroyer once,' said a third sketter, who had dyed her mane blood-red. 'They go very nicely with mint.'

And suddenly, Flax found herself surrounded by a solid wall of stinking fur and sharp claws.

'I've got some mint.' The sketter with the blue beads bent down and bared his teeth at her. 'I've got lots of mint.'

'I – I'm not here about m-mint,' stammered Flax. 'I – I'm here about the—'

'It talks,' interrupted the sketter with the fingerbone necklace. 'It knows words. I've never heard them say anything except, "Help, help, don't eat me!"'

The wall of fur shook with cruel laughter. The claws opened and shut. *Snick. Snick.*

'I'm here about the witch!' shouted Flax.

The laughter stopped. The claws sprang out to their full length.

'What do you know about the witch?' snarled the sketter with the red mane.

'She hasn't finished,' said Flax. 'She wants *more* magic. She wants all the magic in the Floating Forest.'

The sketters threw back their heads and howled

with rage. They stamped their feet, so that soup pots and bones rattled together in a horrible rhythm.

'We'll kill her,' growled the sketter with the blue beads.

'We'll make her into soup,' shouted the one with the red mane.

A chant started up. 'Witch soup, witch soup, witch soup.'

'It won't be easy,' cried Flax, over the noise. 'She's very powerful.'

The chant stopped. The growling started up again.

The sketter with the necklace sneered down at Flax. 'So what do *you* think we should do, little Destroyer?'

Flax gulped. 'I've got a p-plan.'

They laughed. They laughed and laughed and laughed.

And then they listened.

CHAPTER 65
Nothing the Least Bit Tidy

The only forest Rose had ever spent much time in was the one in the royal park.

It was neat and tidy, and an army of gardeners crawled through it on their knees every morning to make sure it *stayed* neat and tidy.

Rose had always thought forests were meant to be like that.

But there was nothing the least bit tidy about the Floating Forest.

It was wild and messy and glorious, and there wasn't a straight line to be seen. Instead, there were winding paths, and moss and spider webs and tangled vines.

Beetles whizzed past Rose's ears. Flies and bees danced around her.

Everything hummed with magic. Especially the trees.

Rose could feel the magic. She could smell it and taste it and *almost* see it.

Being a dragon was so much better than being a queen.

It was also worse. Because when she and the pup came to Minchfold, she knew exactly how much damage her aunt had already done.

She could feel the emptiness of three of the great trees. She could smell it and taste it. She could almost see it.

Aunt Delilah stood beside the empty trees, glowering at the Spellhounds.

'Why is this so much harder than yesterday?' she demanded. 'Give me more of your power.'

'We are giving you all we have,' said the pup's father.

Aunt Delilah snarled with frustration. 'You

think you can stop me? You cannot.'

And she raised her hands to the next tree.

Rose took a deep breath – and let out a wail.

It was shockingly loud.

Aunt Delilah spun around, just as Rose burst out of the trees.

'I'M A MONSTER,' cried Rose. **'OH OH OH! HOW DID THIS HAPPEN? AUNT DELILAH, HELP ME! I DON'T WANT TO BE A MONSTER!'**

And she burst into tears.

Witches are *very* hard to lie to. (Probably because they tell so many lies themselves.)

Fortunately, it was a queen telling *this* lie. A queen *and* a dragon in the same person.

And dragons are almost as good at lying as queens.

CHAPTER 66
The Mor-kits

The mor-kits were a lot smaller than the sketters, and nowhere near as smelly.

But they frightened Flax even more.

They hissed at her. They circled her on silent feet.

They giggled.

Thank you, I am quite aware that a giggle does not sound frightening.

But this was a *hungry* giggle.

A nightmare giggle, full of needle-sharp teeth

and black tongues, and please-run-so-we-can-chase-you.

If you are very lucky, you will never hear a mor-kit giggle. But if you do, I advise you to fall to the ground and pretend you are a stick. If that is too hard, try to look as if you have been dead for some time and are starting to rot.

Mor-kits are fussy eaters and prefer their food fresh.

(Please note that this will not work with sketters. *They* will eat anything. Including sticks.)

Flax was good at pretending to be a stick. But a stick can't summon an army or defeat a witch.

So she stood her ground, and trembled.

'Tasssty,' hissed the mor-kits, as they circled closer.

'Ssscrumptiousss.'

'Sssandwich.'

'I need to t-talk to you,' squeaked Flax. 'About the t-trees. And the w-witch!'

For a moment, she thought they wouldn't listen.

But the mor-kits had seen the dragon tow the Floating Forest through the sky. They had heard the magic being ripped from the trees around Sketterhome. The world was upside down and, for a few minutes at least, they were willing to listen to a minch-wiggin.

(Instead of putting her between slices of a *different* minch-wiggin and calling it a sandwich.)

After the mor-kits, Flax went to the horned globs.

In some ways, they were the hardest of all. Not because they were frightening, but because she kept forgetting they were there, and had to pinch herself over and over as she spoke to them.

After the horned globs, she went looking for the minch-wiggins.

CHAPTER 67
A Proper Spellhound

For the first time in his life, the pup felt enormous.
He was full of rumble and spark, just like a proper
Spellhound.

Best of all, he wasn't scared anymore.

Well...only a little bit.

He was still scared of the witch. And of the
emptiness of the trees whose magic she had stolen.
And of what might happen if Flax couldn't find
an army. Or if the Uncle Edwin dragon didn't
come back in time.

Actually, he was still *really* scared.

But he wasn't going to whimper and put his
paws over his eyes. He was going to *do* something.

Just as soon as he figured out what.

In the clearing, Rose was wailing, **'HELP ME, AUNT! PLEASE!'**

The witch glared at her. 'I told you to eat the cake. A queen is *not* supposed to be a dragon.'

'I'M SORRY, AUNT DELILAH. CAN'T YOU MAKE IT GO AWAY?'

'I am busy. I will deal with you later.' And the witch faced the tree again and raised both her hands.

Rose stomped in front of her. **'BUT WHAT IF I'M STUCK LIKE THIS FOREVER? I WON'T BE ABLE TO SIGN LETTERS. I WON'T BE ABLE TO EAT TRIPE IN WHITE SAUCE WITH THE PRIME MINISTER OF STONEHUFF.'**

'Don't be ridiculous,' the witch said coldly. 'Of course you will not be stuck like that. Now get out of my way.'

'BUT WHAT IF I *AM* STUCK?' cried Rose, not moving.

The witch gave a sigh of irritation. She raised one hand.

'**Reverse!**' she cried.

Nothing happened. Rose was still a dragon.

'**Reverse!**' cried the witch.

Still nothing. The pup suspected that Rose was fighting the witch's spell as hard as she could.

'**OH OH OH, I KNEW IT,**' wailed Rose. '**I'M STUCK!**'

'Nonsense,' snapped the witch. 'I just need a little more power.' And without looking around, she reached for the Spellhounds.

The pup stuck his nose out from the shelter of the trees. The witch didn't see him. But his mother and father did.

They still wore the collars, so they couldn't attack the witch, or escape. But now they knew their son was free, they could back away so she could not draw on their power.

She looked around and saw them. She shrieked at them. She demanded that they come closer.

They refused, though it hurt them dreadfully.

'You think I cannot work without you?' snarled the witch. 'I have power aplenty from the trees I have drained.'

Her eyes flashed.

'𝕽everse!' she shrieked at Rose.

And suddenly the dragon was gone, and Rose was a human girl again, with a ragged coat around her shoulders, and torn pyjama pants.

The witch sniffed. She turned to the oldest tree in Minchfold. She raised her hand—

'Thank you!' cried Rose, throwing herself at the witch and wrapping her arms around her. 'Thank you, Aunt; that was so awful!'

'Control yourself, Felicia,' snarled the witch. 'Queens do *not* hug people.'

She pushed Rose away.

She raised her hand to the tree again—

That's when Flax's army arrived.

CHAPTER 68
Flax's Army

There has never been an army as strange as the one that Flax brought to defend the Floating Forest.

The sketters were at the front, with their claws extended and their hearts full of rage.

Behind them came the mor-kits, giggling and vicious.

Then the horned globs, who everyone else kept treading on, because they forgot they were there.

And last of all, the minch-wiggins, unseen in the shadows.

When the sketters saw the Lady, they flexed their claws. *Snick. Snick.*

They roared their hatred.

Then they poured through the trees towards her.

The witch shouted a **Word**. '**Stop!**'

The sketters kept coming. So did the mor-kits and the horned globs and the minch-wiggins.

'Stuff your ears,' Flax had told them. 'It doesn't matter what you use, as long as it blocks out her voice.'

The minch-wiggins had pine nuts in their ears.

The horned globs had mud.

The mor-kits had grass and fur.

The sketters had—

No, don't ask.

The Lady shouted louder. '**Stop!**'

This time, her **Word** got past some of the blockages. A few of the sketters stopped.

The rest kept coming.

The Lady summoned more of her power.

'𝕾𝖙𝖔𝖕!'

And every single sketter stopped.

Flax, watching from the trees, gasped in dismay.

But the Lady must have aimed her 𝖂𝖔𝖗𝖉 at the sketters and *only* at the sketters. Because the mor-kits, the horned globs and the minch-wiggins kept coming.

The Lady clicked her tongue in irritation. She aimed at the mor-kits.

'𝕾𝖙𝖔𝖕!'

The mor-kits stopped.

But the horned globs and minch-wiggins didn't.

Horned globs do not have hunting teeth, or sharp claws that go *snick snick*. But when the witch forgot them, they threw themselves at her legs until she was knocked to the ground.

Then the minch-wiggins (still in the shadows) wrapped vines around her until she couldn't move.

Flax held her breath. Was this going to work?

Was it really going to *work*?

The short answer is, no.

Oh, you want the long answer?

Very well. But I warn you now, you will not like it.

Because shadows cannot fool a witch for long.

'**Shadows begone!**' cried the Lady, as she lay on the ground wrapped in vines.

And there were the minch-wiggins: Flax's Auntie Grub, her Uncle Beech, her cousin Violet, her brother Bean, and all the rest of them. Blinking at the witch in terror.

They tried to flee, but she shouted, '**Stop!**'

The **Word** got past the pine nuts, and they could not move.

'Undo! Snap! Unravel!' shouted the Lady. And the vines unravelled and snapped and undid.

The Lady tried to stand up. But the horned globs, who she had forgotten again, tucked in their heads and hooves and rolled desperately at her, so she was knocked off her feet once more.

'Remember!' she cried to herself, as she fell. Then, 'Stop!'

The horned globs stopped.

Flax's army had failed.

CHAPTER 69
I am the Lady, and You are Nothing

Flax peered between the trees. Her hand was on her sword. Her heart was thumping.

The pup was there beside her, as hot as a furnace. But she had no magic left, so she couldn't use his power.

Rose was there too, her face pink with anger. 'What can we *do*?' she muttered. 'We have to *do* something.'

But Flax had no ideas left, either.

The Lady stood up and brushed herself down.

All around her, sketters, mor-kits, minch-wiggins and horned globs were frozen to the spot, their eyes full of rage and fear.

The Lady sneered at them. 'You thought you could beat me? I am the Lady, and you are nothing. I will deal with you when I have finished here.'

She raised her hand to the oldest tree in Minchfold—

And Flax thought she heard something in the distance.

Something that sounded like the wind.

Or the rustling of leaves.

Or the sweep of giant wings through the sky...

Flax raced out of the trees with her heart in her mouth and her sword raised. A moment later, the pup dashed after her. So did Rose.

They threw themselves at the witch.

'Death to the Lady!' screamed the sword. 'Probably death to us, too, but definitely death to her!'

And suddenly the pup's parents were howling.

So were the sketters, the mor-kits, the minch-wiggins and the horned globs, all together, so that hardly anything else could be heard.

The Lady swiped Flax and the sword aside with one blow of her hand. She threw off Rose. She tried to grab hold of the pup, crying, 'I will use *your* power!'

The pup bit her.

Now the witch howled, too. 'I will kill you all,' she shrieked.

She raised her hands, just as a dragon with red-gold scales and spikes all the way down his back plunged out of the sky.

At the very last minute, the Lady saw him coming. She opened her mouth to say a 𝔀𝓸𝓻𝓭—

CHAPTER 70
Sleeping Dragons

There is an old saying in Hallow: 'Let sleeping dragons lie.'

The witch should have taken note of it.

But she did not.

She murdered my sister, Queen Alyss, and her husband, Prince Malik, when Felicia was six months old. Their bodies were never found, but there was blood aplenty, and we knew they must be dead.

The witch started a rumour that they had been taken by a dragon.

But I never suspected her, not once.

Instead, I trusted her.

I trusted her so much that I told her the Three Great Secrets, because another person needed to know them in case something happened to me. And Felicia was too young.

The witch swore that the Secrets would be safe with her.

She waited until Felicia was two years old. Then she came upon me in the palace, while I was asleep in my human form. She had the collar around my neck before I knew what was happening.

I fought against that cursed collar with all my strength. And at first, I could resist it, just as the Spellhounds resisted theirs. I could not escape, but I could lie to my jailer. To my turnkey.

For years, I managed to persuade her that the Floating Forest moved around, and its whereabouts were a mystery even to me.

But the longer I wore the collar, the more her will overcame mine. Until one day, I could no longer lie.

That was when she sent me to steal the Spellhounds.

And the Floating Forest.

My rage had been growing for eight long years. So it was no surprise at all that, there in the heart of Minchfold, I lost my temper.

I was no longer hungry; I had a cow and two sheep in my belly.

So I suppose I could have imprisoned the witch, as she had imprisoned me.

But really, it was much simpler to just – eat her.

CHAPTER 71
Destroyer-of-Dragons

As the Lady disappeared down the dragon's gullet, the collars fell from the necks of the Spellhounds. The sketters, mor-kits, horned globs and minch-wiggins discovered that they could move again.

Everyone started to rejoice...

Until the dragon licked his lips.

The sketters flinched and snarled. The mor-kits hissed. The horned globs became more forgettable than ever.

But the minch-wiggins pushed Auntie Grub towards Flax, whispering, 'Tell her, Grub. She's got to do it. Now!'

Auntie Grub teetered from one foot to the

other. She straightened her whiskers. She cleared her throat. (Very quietly.)

'Now you must destroy the dragon,' she whispered to Flax. 'Quickly, while he's resting.'

Flax blinked at her. 'But he saved us. He saved the Floating Forest. He ate the witch.'

'And next he will eat us,' hissed Auntie Grub. 'It's what dragons *do*. So you must get in first. Destroyer-of-Dragons isn't just a nice title, you know. It's your job. It's your duty!'

The dragon raised his head, as if he had caught the edge of the conversation. He beckoned to Flax with an enormous claw. **'I DON'T THINK WE HAVE BEEN PROPERLY INTRODUCED, LITTLE MINCH-WIGGIN.'**

Auntie Grub gave Flax a shove. 'Go on.'

Flax took a cautious step towards the dragon. She tilted her head and gazed up at him. 'My name is F–Flaxseed, sir.'

'And the rest,' hissed Auntie Grub, from a safe distance.

'No,' whispered Flax.

'Yes,' insisted Auntie Grub. She raised her voice. 'Not *just* Flaxseed. She's Destroyer-of-Dragons-and-Protector-of-her-People.'

'So don't try any funny business, dragon,' shouted Cousin Violet. 'She's got a famous sword and a satchel full of magic.'

The dragon lowered his head until the end of his enormous nose almost touched Flax. A puff of steam surrounded her.

'IS THIS TRUE? DO YOU HAVE A SATCHEL FULL OF MAGIC?'

Flax thought about lying.

And decided not to.

'N-no, sir. I only ever had a little bit.'

There was a buzz of voices behind her as her relatives exclaimed in shock and dismay.

But the dragon said, **'THAT IS WHAT I THOUGHT. YOU DO NOT NEED MUCH MAGIC AT ALL TO SUMMON A DRAGON.'**

'To *summon* a dragon?' squeaked Flax.

'PERHAPS YOU PREFER THE WORD "SIGNAL". OR "CALL"? OR "WARN"?'

'B–but why would I want to call a dragon?'

Uncle Edwin sat back on his haunches. **'WHEN I GAVE THE SATCHEL TO YOUR MANY-TIMES-GREAT-GRANDMOTHER—'**

'*You* gave her the satchel?' squeaked Flax. 'But – but – but *why*? And what about the sword?'

'I DO NOT RECOGNISE THE SWORD,' said the dragon. **'ONE OF YOUR ANCESTORS MUST HAVE FOUND IT.'**

'Told you so,' whispered the sword.

'AS FOR WHY, IT IS MY DUTY AS A DRAGON OF HALLOW TO GUARD THE FLOATING FOREST. AND SINCE I COULD NOT ALWAYS BE HERE, I NEEDED SOMEONE TO WARN ME IF A WITCH CAME SNIFFING AROUND. SOMEONE WITH EXCELLENT HEARING, WHO KNEW EVERY PART OF

THE FOREST. WHO BETTER THAN A MINCH-WIGGIN?'

He bowed his head again. **'YOU WERE NEVER MEANT TO BE DESTROYER-OF-DRAGONS, LITTLE ONE. YOU WERE MEANT TO BE *CALLER*-OF-DRAGONS. THAT IS WHAT THE MAGIC WAS FOR; TO CALL ME IF EVER A WITCH APPEARED IN THE FOREST. BUT SOMEWHERE OVER THE YEARS, THE ORIGINAL WORD WAS LOST AND CHANGED.'**

Flax's head swam. 'So – so I never needed a lot of magic? I never needed the sword?'

'Now hang on a minute,' said the sword.

'NO,' said the dragon. **'BUT IT WAS JUST AS WELL YOU HAD IT.'**

'Thank you,' muttered the sword. 'At least *someone* appreciates me.'

It was too much to take in all at once, especially after everything else that had happened.

Flax sat down rather quickly.

After a moment, the pup came and sat beside her.

So did Rose.

Flax leaned against them and closed her eyes.

She could hear Auntie Grub telling everyone that *she* had always known it was supposed to be Caller, not Destroyer, and that she was surprised no one else had realised.

She could hear the sketters arguing (very quietly) about whether it was possible to make soup out of a dragon, and the mor-kits giggling (even more quietly) about dragon sandwiches.

She could hear the frogs croaking and the birds singing—

And the deep, slow song of the trees of the Floating Forest.

We saved them, she thought. *We saved nearly all of them.*

Above her head, Rose said, 'Uncle Edwin, I don't want to go back to being Felicia. Can I be Rose from now on?'

'OF COURSE,' said her uncle. 'SO WHAT DO YOU THINK WE SHOULD DO NOW, ROSE?'

'We should put everything back the way it's supposed to be,' said Rose.

And so we come to the end of our story.

Which is also a new beginning.

CHAPTER 72
In a Quiet Corner of Hallow

In a quiet corner of Hallow, far from cities and towns, roads and railways, walls and witches, there lives a family of Spellhounds.

Yes, the Floating Forest is back in its proper place. My niece and I towed it there under cover of darkness, cheered on by hundreds of minch-wiggins, mor-kits, sketters and horned globs.

Yes, the pup is back with his parents, who are as proud of him as can be.

Though no one calls him pup anymore. They call him He-Who-Brings-Thunder-Inside-the-Mountain.

Or Thunder, for short.

Yes, Rose is still Queen of Hallow. (And I am Regent once again.)

She still signs letters. But now they are about building homes for the children who sleep in the gutter, and finding jobs for one-legged soldiers.

She has a puppy with a cute little nose and bright black eyes, small enough to sit on her lap when she rides in the back of the royal automobile.

And between us, we guard the Three Great Secrets of Hallow.

The First Great Secret is that Queen Rose is a dragon.

The Second Great Secret is that the Floating Forest is the very heart of Hallow.

The Third Great Secret is the Spellhounds.

Remember not to tell *anyone*.

Now I must leave you. It is the Queen's bedtime, and I have promised her a story about her parents.

(I have also promised that she need never eat tripe again. And that she can re-hire the dressmakers Mansie Undercroft and Dashy Slove.)

What's that? You're wondering what happened to Flax?

She is living in the Floating Forest, of course.

With her satchel, which I restocked with just enough magic to summon a dragon.

And her sword, which becomes a cake knife whenever Rose visits.

And her keen ears, which will listen for witches for the rest of her life.

Good night, Flax.

Good night, brave little minch-wiggin.

Good night, Caller-of-Dragons.

Acknowledgements

Huge thanks to all the wonderful people at Allen & Unwin who helped turn my manuscript into a real book, especially Anna McFarlane who could, entirely by herself, face down an army of sketters, and Kate Whitfield, who would have serious words with the mor-kits about their definition of a sandwich.

Thanks as always to my brilliant agent, Margaret Connolly, whose advice is worth its weight in minch-wiggins.

Thanks to dramaturg Peter Matheson for his generous help and keen eye, to Hannah Janzen for another of her beautiful designs, and to

Sally Soweol Han for the gorgeous illustrations.

And lastly, thanks to my writing group, to whom this book is dedicated. When I showed them the very beginning of the very first uncertain draft, they said, 'Give us more of the narrator!'

So I did.

About the Author

LIAN TANNER has worked as a teacher, a tourist bus driver, a freelance journalist, a juggler, an editor and a professional actor. She has been dynamited while scuba diving and arrested while busking. She once spent a week in the jungles of Papua New Guinea, searching for a Japanese soldier left over from the Second World War. It took her a while to realise that all this was preparation for becoming a writer. Nowadays Lian lives by the sea in southern Tasmania.